¿Eres Tú? is a work of fiction. All incidents and dialogue, and all characters, with the exception of some well-known historical and public figures, are products of the author's imagination. In all other respects, any resemblance to persons living or dead in entirely coincidental.

Published in the United States by Book Shelf Editions, Winona, Minnesota, a division of The Book Shelf, LLP Independent Booksellers.

ISBN 978-1944008-55-0

Cover design by Matt Stauffer.

¿Eres tú?

A novel of Lonquimay

By

Frank H. Tainter

To Carol,
we hope you enjoy
this novel.
Frank & Malena

Foreword

This novel is fiction and most of the characters in this story are fictional. However, many of the individual events described here actually happened either to the author or to members of his immediate or extended family. The major historical events are true and provide a backdrop around which this story is woven. The timing of a few historical events was changed to better fit the narrative.

A born and bred true native Chilean might have preferred a different slant on the history and examples than what the author has chosen to present, and may wonder about the strange assemblage of adventures that are presented. Suffice it to say that the *gringo* author has attempted to present this narrative as seen mainly through the eyes of Robert, our hero, and, to a lesser extent, through the eyes of our heroine, *Rosa*. It is basically the adventure of a foreigner who knows little about Chile, but who has come to work and, eventually, live in Chile.

This novel is written primarily in English, which is printed in normal font style. Spanish and Latin words and phrases are printed in italics. All the Spanish words are presented in italics. There are a few words in the dialect of the native Chileans living in the area of the story, the *Pehuenches*. These are presented in bold font style. An example is **Foye**, a medicinal plant name. In Spanish it is called *canelo*.

This novel makes considerable reference to medicinal plants and includes a list in the appendix of some of these plants and their supposed remedies. The reader should be aware that most medicinal plants have not been rigorously tested for their efficacy by modern scientific techniques against illness or disease. However, any potential critic must consider that while modern medicine has only been around for a little over a century, medicinal plants have been used by countless individuals on several continents over a period of many thousands of years. Would these people have continued to use something that had no positive effect? The answer to that question makes a strong argument in the sense that perhaps medicinal plants with historical usage do have some authentic medicinal value.

At any rate, anyone contemplating the use of medicinal plants should first consult with their doctor. As recent research has shown, many of the medicinal plants listed in this novel have subsequently been found to have extremely powerful medicinal effects. When the hero of this novel began his exploratory work in the 1960s, general public interest in medicinal plants was only local at best. At the time this novel was written (2015), there has been an incredible upsurge in the acceptance, use, and commercialization of medicinal plants, and scientific testing has revealed efficacious chemical components in certain plants.

At the beginning of most chapters there is either a title or short verse of a piece of music from Chilean folklore that the author has chosen in order to convey a sense of the emotion to be experienced in that chapter. To set the stage for that chapter and help the reader gain a complete experience of what the author has tried to convey, it would be helpful for the reader to listen to the suggested music before reading that chapter.

The inspiration for this novel came quite literally during a night flight from *Santiago*, Chile on October 23, 2013. Sleep came in fits during that night. The plane was nearly full, and the uncomfortable seats allowed only fitful sleep, and then joint aches from sitting in one position or other caused the author to awaken in a stupor. During those moments of stupor this entire story came to the author almost as if he were reading it from memory and with such clarity that even months later he could recall each and every detail of it.

Dedication

This book is dedicated to *Ramón Rosende*. He was my Chilean counterpart when I served in the Peace Corps and was a good friend and a true Chilean. Shortly after the military coup in 1973 he shared the national soccer stadium with *Víctor Jara*, and was to be executed because he was a socialist. However, his life was saved by the intervention of a retired army general named *Jorge Beroíza*. Mr. *Beroíza* was the fiscal agent at the *Instituto Forestal* where *Ramón Rosende* worked. Mr. *Beroíza* was not sympathetic to the cause of the military coup but because of his military experience, he successfully argued on behalf of

Ramón Rosende, Oscar Wetling, Germán Tamm, and other former employees of the *Instituto* who had been arrested and were to be executed.

After three months in the national soccer stadium, *Ramón Rosende* was released, now reduced to skin and bone, and infested with lice. When he arrived at his home, his wife, a medical doctor, informed him that she had arranged for safe passage, and work, for the both of them in Venezuela. *Ramón* stood in the door, crossed his arms and

Ramón Rosende with his sons, *Ramón* (left) and *Pablito* (Christmas, 1964).

declared, "I am a Chilean, I was born here, and I will die here." He lived several more years but had a fatal heart attack at the wedding of one of his sons. In the final analysis, he loved Chile more than his life. He didn't know it but he shared much of this love with me.

The price that some people have to pay for being a good citizen in their country of birth is a weird thing. *Ramón Rosende's* father had been an ambassador to Italy and was later a candidate for the Chilean presidency. He ran as a popular socialist. Just before the election, unknown members of the opposition poisoned him.

Gratitude

This novel would have not been possible without the support of my wife, *María Magdalena*. And she would want the reader to know that this is not how we did it.

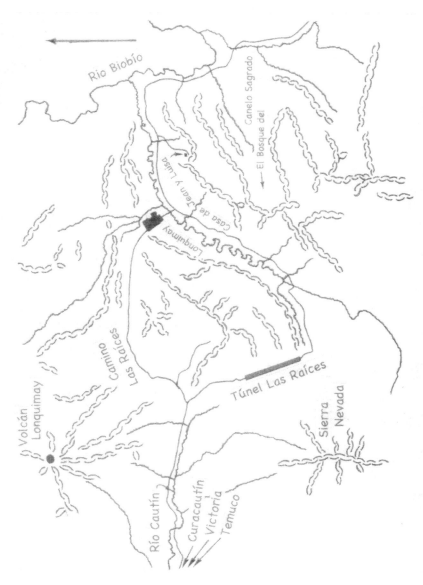

The area of our story.

Chapter 1
Lonquimay Valley, Chile
November, 1980

"Rosa colorada." (The red rose.) – Title of song from Chilean folklore.

This story centers on a small village, *Lonquimay*, in south-central Chile. The name *Lonquimay*, or **Lonkimay**, has two possible meanings. In the original native tongue the name means *"bosque tupido"* (dense forest) or *"cabeza del río"* (river basin). Either could be true since both describe the area in near-prehistoric times. Before illegal logging and uncontrolled wild fires in the mountains surrounding the village destroyed most of them, extensive and dense forests of Araucaria pines blanketed the region. The village is also just down river from the source of the *Naranjo* River that is a tributary to the *Río Biobío*, a major river of Chile, and for many centuries, a border between the invading Incas and the later invading Spaniards.

The village of *Lonquimay* is near the head of a long valley of the same name. It is a long, broad valley that begins about halfway between the cities of *Victoria* and *Temuco*. The valley follows the *Cautín* River as it meanders its way down from the Andes Mountains. The valley crosses the *Cordillera*, becoming an inter-mountain plateau, and then forms another valley that winds back down into Argentina on the eastern side of the Andean *Cordillera*. More will be said later to describe the area and the people living there.

It was a bright, crisp, spring day in the valley, with an intense blue sky and, although the nights were still cool, the days had begun to warm quickly. The landscape vegetation was in early full bloom. It was mid-November and the intense-scarlet flowers of the *fosforito* trees formed large and small splotches of intense color in the view from the road. Along fences and the edges of fields there were individual trees

1

with the bright scarlet flowers and large patches of the same trees in the native forest on the hillsides on either side of the road. The most plentiful tree component of this forest was *ñire*, one of the deciduous southern beeches, which was just beginning to leaf out and its new leaves lent a light-green color to the landscape.

The globose witches' brooms of the bright yellow/gold-colored parasitic plant called *misodendrum* were just beginning to be partially obscured by the unfolding leaves of the *ñire*. This combination of colors produced splotches of dark green, light green, and bright scarlet against the massive dark green-cloaked mountains. A light dusting of black volcanic sand drifted across the road in the morning breeze and several condors lazily circled overhead.

A closer examination looking westward down the valley revealed that a car was traveling eastward up the valley road. The car wove its way along the crooked gravel road and finally came close to the crest at the upper end of the valley, raising a faint trail of dust as it putted and bounced along. The main subject of our story, Robert, had rented the green 1947 Jeep station wagon in *Santiago*.

Oddly, it was the same vehicle he had used almost ten years earlier during his medicinal plant hunting forays. Older vehicles were difficult to find now that the Pinochet military regime had outlawed them from service. They were thought to be an embarrassment in an advanced country like Chile. Trucks older than 10 years of age were removed from the road almost immediately after the coup, but automobiles were only beginning to be subjected to the new ruling. The owner said this would be the last time that Robert could use this car and after this trip he would not be able to renew the license.

It felt good to be back in Chile and, as Robert drove along, a flood of disjunctive memories flashed through his mind, each occupying only a second or two of his thoughts. Some he didn't want to think about but they forced their way into his head anyway. Each time he shifted gears, though, he had to leave his reverie. The clutch and standard transmission had caused him considerable discomfort as

2

he had not previously driven in a standard transmission vehicle with his newly acquired artificial left leg.

After six years in a coma, his physical rehabilitation had been extremely difficult and any physical exertion caused extreme discomfort and very quickly developed into a general debilitating fatigue. He could will his leg to depress the clutch pedal but repeated clutch work made the left leg muscle seem to have turned into jelly. Then he reminded himself as to why he was here and he willed himself to ignore the pain and move on.

After he left *Santiago* he had taken a hurried trip down the Pan American Highway to *Victoria*, although he stopped at nearly every service station to sample the fresh fruits and juice drinks. He particularly liked fresh strawberry juice, and there was a lot of it at each stop as the strawberries had begun to mature a few days before his arrival. During his earlier time in Chile, he had also enjoyed watermelon juice but on this trip it was much too early for watermelons. At *Victoria* he had turned eastward onto the secondary road that penetrated approximately 78 miles up the *Lonquimay* Valley and toward the Andean *Cordillera*.

Nearing the head end of the valley the road came to a junction. Either road led to the village of *Lonquimay*. Robert chose to take the *Camino Las Raíces* road. In winter this road was impassable because of heavy snow but now, in spring, the road had been recently plowed and was free of snow. In winter the only road passage to *Lonquimay* was through the *Túnel Las Raíces*, at that time the longest tunnel in South America. It was constructed for a railway line during the 1930s but it had been abandoned for that purpose and now was the only all-weather road to *Lonquimay*.

As the terrain rose in elevation, he entered the zone of pure Araucaria pine forests and he recalled the majesty and beauty of these trees, each with dark green foliage forming an umbrella-shaped crown that complemented the tall, nearly black branchless trunk. These, in turn, contrasted with the deep blue sky above them with scattered

3

white cottony clouds. Araucaria pines dated from the time of the dinosaurs and the larger trees were several hundreds to over a thousand years of age. Although many had been logged or burned, some areas still retained a lot of the majestic pines.

Although the Araucaria pines were considered sacred by the *Pehuenche* natives, the military regime had encouraged land grabbing on the *Pehuenche* lands and some logging of these sacred trees was still being conducted by these illegal land colonizers. Along the road, Robert passed several teams of oxen, each team slogging along pulling a wooden-wheeled cart, with each carrying a single, large Araucaria pine log. Some logs were over three feet in diameter. Further along several drovers herded a flock of sheep and Robert waited as they passed by on the road.

The drive up the valley was nostalgic for Robert, but as he began to relive the memories of some of his work and experiences there, he also began to feel emotional. He recalled the last time he was here in this valley, about the joy he felt performing his work and his medicinal plant collections, about the *González* family, *Claudia* and *Juan*, descendants of *Pehuenche* natives who had helped him a great deal with his collection of medicinal plants. He also thought about their daughter, *Rosa*, who hadn't seemed to like him very much, except for those last few days he had been with the family as he packed his plant materials and prepared to leave Chile.

The *González* family, *Rosa's* mother *Claudia* and her father *Juan*, and her older brother *Miguel*, had a small sheep and cattle ranch that had been in the family since their grandparents had fled to the valley from the Argentine side of the Andes Mountains during the *Rojas* campaign to exterminate the native aborigines.

The *Gonzálezes* were probably a little more well-to-do than many of their neighbors, partially because of the moderate wealth of some of their ancestors, and because they also supplemented their subsistence ranch income by preserving and singing folk songs at various events and celebrations around Chile. They were well known as folk singers and respected because they made great efforts to seek out and preserve Chilean folk music, especially that of the Araucanian natives of all of southern Chile. They had even gone on tour in Europe and had cut a number of records.

Claudia was also a respected **machi**, a person with a great knowledge of medicinal plants. She was not a practicing **machi** but, rather, spent her energies preserving ancestral knowledge of those remedies. Robert really enjoyed the time he spent with the *González* family and now he was recalling, when he was in a coma, the vision of *Claudia* imploring him to return to Chile and help *Rosa*. He could think of no reason why he should be needed.

Robert's thoughts were abruptly interrupted again by another vision of *Claudia* and he didn't want to think about jumping into the cold, muddy river to save her life, but he could not put that thought out of his mind. He remembered the little dog that heroically jumped into the water and tried to save his mistress but was caught in the swift current and dragged under some floating branches and drowned. He reflected at the extreme emotions they all felt after the team of oxen had pulled the tree off *Claudia* and many hands pulled both of them out of the river and up onto the bank and everyone realized that she would be all right. That happiness was severely tempered, though, by the loss of their faithful dog.

Shortly before that day, in mid-1973, he had received his draft notice and had only a few weeks in which to settle his affairs and return to the States. So, several days later, after he had bid farewell to the family, and as he was driving down the valley he passed through a street fair in *Curacautín* and saw a vender with several puppies for sale. On an impulse he stopped and watched the puppies for a long time.

As they rolled and wrestled around, one, a yellow Labrador, looked up and saw Robert standing there. The dog sat down and continued to watch Robert for a while and then tried to walk toward him, pulling on her little leash in the little cluster of tumbling puppies. She again sat down but kept wagging her tail to her right side as she watched Robert, for some unknown reason very interested in this *gringo*. Robert finally walked over, pulled out his wallet and asked, *"¿Cuánto vale?"* The man answered, *"Cinco escudos."* He handed the money to the vender, who was surprised when Robert didn't even try to negotiate a lower price.

So, he put the dog in the back of the Jeep and turned around and headed back up the valley. Two hours later he again turned into the driveway and pulled up to the *González* house. As he opened the car door, the surprised family came out onto the porch and he heard *Rosa* say, "Uh huh, so the *gringo* can't leave his Chilean family, huh? He wants to steal more of our magical plant remedies."

Robert put the puppy under his arm and walked up to the porch and handed it to *Claudia*. "Here," he said, "A little something to remember me by." As he left for the second time he noticed that this time everyone had tears in their eyes. As he got into the car he heard *Rosa* say with a choked voice, "Hurry back *gringo*."

He was finally able to push that thought out of his mind but it was immediately replaced by another day, in late 1973 in Vietnam, when he thought he saw, and heard, the vision of a much younger *Claudia* imploring him to save the Vietnamese family trapped in the middle of a fire fight. He often relived both of these visions and would awake with his heart pounding and his clothes drenched with sweat. He couldn't understand the significance of that experience or why he thought he had seen her there. Today we might conclude that he suffered from a type of post-traumatic stress syndrome.

It took him quite awhile to recover from his experience in Vietnam and dealing with the loss of his leg plus getting used to the prosthetic limb. He also still had some pretty brutal trauma that made his transition back into a somewhat normal life very slow at times. After awakening from six years in a coma he had worked on his physical rehabilitation with a passion as he recalled the dream he thought he had of *Claudia*, telling him that *Rosa* needed help.

Robert could have lived a relatively decent life on his disability pension, but he wanted to get back to his plant work and renew the joy that he had experienced earlier as a plant explorer and collector, especially in Chile. His former partner at Pharmtec had urged Robert to return to Chile and resume some of his collecting attempts, at least on a trial basis. If it didn't work out he could still return to the company and work at the desk or at a laboratory job.

As he pushed these thoughts out of his mind, he looked out the open driver's window at the *Lonquimay* Volcano on his left and deeply inhaled the fresh air with just a hint of the odors of the last of the melting snow on the volcano's flanks, and *cilantro*, a common herb used as a food flavoring. He thought about some of the plants he had collected, some of the medications extracted from them, and the day when he had stopped at the *González* farm to ask for permission to collect on their land. They had certainly helped him a lot and Robert's boss had subsequently developed a plan for a *Pehuenche* cooperative to be compensated for their help. He wondered if they would remember him, if *Rosa* had married and moved away, if the little dog he gave them was still around. Was *Rosa* in some kind of trouble as his vision of *Claudia* had intimated?

His heart beat a little faster as he turned south onto the winding secondary road into their ranch, and then he stopped as he saw that the bridge crossing the creek was washed out. He could see their house nearly a mile or so up the side road, nestled in the base of a narrow valley. He parked and climbed out. As he walked along the road toward the washout he inhaled the familiar scents of the land, the earthy odor of new plant growth, the dried sheep manure, and the faint spicy scent of dried plants from last year's growth. Overhead, the perpetual condors circled and wheeled around in an air updraft.

As he approached the washout and began to walk down into the ravine, he noticed that the house and yard in general seemed to be in terrible repair, far worse than when he had left. He noticed someone, a woman perhaps, on the shed roof pounding on the sheet metal roof with a hammer. He could see that she had long, black hair but he couldn't see well enough to determine if that was *Rosa*. He saw her suddenly drop the hammer and then heard her curse, *"¡Ay, miercoles! ¡Me pegué en un dedo!"*, (Oops, Darn! I hit my finger!), and put her finger in her mouth. Could that be *Rosa*? He had never heard her swear!

He crossed the creek by jumping from rock to rock and just as he had begun to climb back out onto the far bank, a young girl came running from the back of the house into the front yard, throwing a stick for a dog to fetch. Suddenly, the dog saw him and started barking, and began to run toward him. He wondered if it was the same dog he had given to *Rosa's* mother. It was grown now and the same color but this one was missing a hind leg.

The girl abruptly stopped when she saw Robert and called for the dog as it ran toward Robert. Then she dropped the stick and ran over to the shed and shouted to the woman on the roof, *"¡Mamá, Mamá, alguien viene!"* (Mommy, mommy, someone is coming!) The woman turned to look, and looked for a few long moments, still with her finger in her mouth. Then she climbed down the ladder and stood by the girl.

As Robert got closer, noticeably limping as the stump of his missing leg was hurting a great deal, the woman's hand went to her mouth, she gasped, and hugged the girl closer. It was *Rosa*! She was a little thinner than he remembered but still had the long, black hair and the aquiline features that he had grown so fond of although he never did find the courage to tell her. And her brown eyes were flashing at him now! Robert could see those flashing eyes very clearly now. She, the girl, and the dog just stood there, watching Robert hobbling toward them with his one good leg and his other, artificial leg.

As Robert approached, the dog ran up to him barking fiercely as if its jaw were going to fall off. Then, she suddenly stopped a dozen feet away and just sat down and looked at Robert, panting, tilting her head, and with her tail wagging, toward her right side. Robert again wondered if this could be the same dog he had given to *Claudia*. The dog tilted her head from side to side and whimpered, and seemed to be questioning itself as if it might have recognized him. *Rosa* and the girl walked up behind the dog. *Rosa's* hand held the girl's hand tightly.

Robert's gaze briefly flashed over to the *Lonquimay* Volcano over his right shoulder, then his eyes began to mist over as he heard the girl ask, *"¿Mamá, porqué estás llorando? Por favor no llores. ¿Qué pasa?"* (Mommy, why are you crying? Please don't cry. What's the matter?). Robert's heart sank as he realized that *Rosa* must be married and that this young girl was her daughter. *Rosa* and Robert just stood looking at each other for several more long seconds.

Then she placed her hands on her checks, gasped, and asked, *"¿Eres tú? ¿Roberto, eres realmente tú?"* (Is it you? *Roberto*, is it really you?) Then, as tears began to roll down her cheeks, she looked down at the girl and said, *"¡Paulinita, este hombre desgraciado es tu papá!"* Robert remembered enough Spanish to understand what she had said. *"Paulina*, this nasty man is your father!"

After that shock, he thought that perhaps he should just turn around and leave, but then she said *"¡Y estoy tan feliz de verlo nuevamente!"* (And I'm so happy to see him again!). *Rosa* and Robert just stood looking at each other again for another long second. Then, she, and the dog, ran toward him, jumped on him and they all fell down in a wild embrace of arms and legs, dog paws, her black hair, and their tears.

Robert was back in Chile, and alive again!

Araucaria pine trees
(redrawn from Chile Stamp #708)

Chapter 2
To a New Land
At Least 13,400 Years Before the Present

"Soy de la sangre Araucana." (I am of Araucanian blood.) – Song verse
from Chilean/*Mapuche* folklore.

The history of human involvement in what was to eventually become known in the present day as the *Lonquimay* Valley began at least 13,400 years ago when people arrived on the American continent. The ancestors of the modern day *González* family were part of a small band of men, women, children, and dogs. They were trekking southward in a mountain valley, approximately 100 miles north of what is now Yellowstone National Park in the present state of Montana. We know this today because they left traces of their passage.

They carried weapons with a characteristically shaped stone head that would later become known as the Clovis point. The Clovis point was a well-crafted and beautiful stone spearhead and arrowhead. It was designed for killing large animals such as the wooly mammoth and the American mastodon. However, this particular projectile point style was used for only a relatively short time, appearing suddenly with the Clovis people as they would later become known, and then disappearing from history just as suddenly, for reasons which we will soon see.

The story of this band actually began around 50,000 years before, when their ancestors arrived in Europe following a long trek from Africa. That journey had begun 200,000 years earlier, by which time modern *Homo sapiens* had evolved. Around 160,000 years ago, climate conditions had deteriorated, leaving inland Africa too dry and uninhabitable. By the time these people arrived in Europe they were true *H. sapiens* and thrived there after they had become accomplished invasive predators.

These early humans had also formed a symbiotic relationship with the wolf ancestors of modern-day dogs. Many large animals such as cave bears became extinct at about that time in Europe and it is believed that their demise was a direct result of these new, highly efficient hunting partners. There has been some speculation that another race of primitive people, the Neanderthals, became extinct at this same time because they could not compete with these new, more efficient, hunters.

Genetic and archeological evidence indicates that, around some 32,000 years ago, these humans had moved from Europe, into Siberia, and then into northwestern Beringia. Subsequently, between 26,000 and 18,000 years ago, they went into eastern Beringia, ready for the trek across the land bridge. There is some archeological evidence that a few may have migrated as early as 32,000 years ago, during one of the interglacial epochs before the Pleistocene when the land bridge would also have been exposed. However, subsequent genetic mutations in the later and larger group, our group, left unique DNA markers that were found only in what were soon to become Native Americans.

Based on evidence gathered from archeological, genomic, mitochondrial DNA, and Y-chromosome DNA, there were only three major migration events into the prehistoric Americas. Our group was among the first arrivals. Two later migrations from Siberia peopled the northwestern regions of what is now Canada and part of western North America. These migrants concentrated in northern Canada and are the ancestors of the Intuits. Another group migrated into west-central Canada. All the groups came with their dogs. The dogs, which were becoming more and more domesticated, continued to give early humans a great advantage for survival because they allowed them to track smaller animals such as deer, and to corral and harass big-game animals, and then kill them with their spears. For a time they may have served as food for their masters, but they also probably helped carry meat of recently-killed animals to the next camping site.

All of these immigrants came during the time of the Pleistocene glaciation, traveling along the Beringian land bridge, created by lowering of the oceans as a great deal of ocean water was tied up in the form of glacier ice. This land bridge connected Siberia with Alaska. The frigid climate was quite inhospitable to humans and the newcomers traveled quickly southward mainly along the coast of western North America. Genetic evidence also suggests that perhaps less than a total of 5,000 individuals dispersed across the bridge and then southward.

The new arrivals were constantly on the move. The harsh climate precluded gaining much sustenance from the meager plant life, mainly from tundra species, and so they were forced to depend exclusively on hunting animals for their food. At the time, the vegetation was arctic in nature and not very diverse. Later research would reveal that much of arctic vegetation consisted of dry steppe-tundra type dominated not by grass but by herbaceous vascular plants. By the time of the glacial maximum (25-15,000 years before the present), plant diversity had declined markedly. When the later moist tundra appeared it was dominated by a more diverse assemblage of woody plants and grasses that promoted a different group of herbivores. One of the earliest medicinal plants they undoubtedly encountered was horsetail, a very primitive plant that was useful for polishing objects because of its high silica content. It had some medicinal properties as well.

Small animals did not provide enough sustenance for a group of hungry people constantly on the move, although small animals and fish undoubtedly supplemented some of their food needs. Large animals were needed to provide the considerable amount of fresh meat needed to survive in the frozen environment. In the tundra the new immigrants hunted the large animals already mentioned, the wooly mammoth, the typical tundra elephant, and farther south, the American mastodon, a spruce-eating elephant that also lived at that same time but in a different and slightly more favorable environment.

As each successive generation of migrants passed farther south, and eastward, into their new home, they pursued the larger animals and were quite successful in causing their scarcity. In only a few generations they caused the extinction of the large animals, and the Clovis point, which was designed to kill these large animals, was no longer useful on the smaller game animals. Then the Folsom point was developed for hunting the smaller animals, especially the American bison.

The members of the group had not eaten in several days and were hungry. Today they were following the trail of an American mastodon, as they had been doing for the past several days. The mastodon knew it was being followed and was succumbing to their hunter/gatherer strategy. The dogs were constantly harassing the animal. They would worry the animal or wear it down physically until it would finally make a stand. Then they would attack the animal from all sides, with the men, women, and older children attempting to spear the lower parts of the mastodon with their Clovis-tipped spears. The animal was pushed to further frenzy by the dozen or so barking and snarling dogs nipping at its heels.

If one of the hunters was successful, he was able to sever one of the hamstrings in the lower leg. This reduced the animal's mobility and, as it became fear-crazed, the animal started making mistakes in its defense. This was when it was most dangerous. Another method of attack was for a person to run underneath the animal and stab it in the belly. If the hole was large enough, the animal's intestines would burst out of the hole and trip the animal, or it would slowly bleed to death, or become weakened or slowed enough to be dispatched by other means.

Attacking a large animal like a mastodon was a risky business and seldom was there an attack event that did not result in injury or death to at least some of the hunters. On the other hand, if a hunt was successful, the enormous quantity of fresh meat that resulted ensured that the band would survive for several more weeks.

In the colder weather, the band would load up as much meat as they could carry and continue their southward trek. Somewhere during their southward march they learned to dry the meat during the drier summers to produce jerky, which then also allowed them to survive longer periods between hunts.

Hunting of large animals such as mastodons was relatively easier in one sense as these large animals were not able to run very far for long distances and they could be successfully pursued and eventually stopped. The mammoths and mastodons, the wooly rhinoceros, and the wild horse all fell to the Clovis points of their spears and arrows.

As these larger animals became scarce so too did their predators such as the American lion and the saber-toothed tiger. There simply wasn't enough large game for both the humans, and the other large predators, to hunt and survive. The hunt by the Clovis people for other more plentiful smaller animals such as deer or antelope was successful but required more time spent in chasing and stalking, or cunning, and it provided less food for the amount of time invested in the hunt.

Later, the hunters also used the bow and arrow, the atlatl, and still later, when in South America, the *boleodoras*. Deer and elk were particularly desired as so many tools could be made from the antlers and bones, and clothes from the hides. Grizzly bears were often encountered but were not killed unless the migrants were forced to by the enraged bear. The migrants were efficient killing machines. As big game became sparse in a particular area, they moved on, usually southward but sometimes eastward.

The sharpest extinction of mammals occurred at the end of the Pleistocene glaciation. Over 39 genera of large animals disappeared in less than 3,000 years, including mammoths, mastodons, camels, llamas, two genera of deer, woodland musk oxen, two genera of pronghorns, stag-moose, shrub-oxen, horses and giant beavers.

We know that our group passed through what is now central Montana around 13,000 years ago, because one of their members, a 1-year-old baby boy, died and was buried where he died, on land now belonging to the Anzick family. The grave was discovered by accident in 1968 by construction workers.

The distinctive spear points and other items buried with him show that the boy belonged to the Clovis people who arrived in the area of present day Montana roughly 13,000 years ago. This Anzick boy, named for the present-day family that owns the land, is the only known Clovis burial. Clovis culture was widespread between 13,000 and 12,600 years ago and within a few generations the only presently recognized relics from their culture, the finely crafted Clovis spear and arrow points, ceased being made and, except for the genetic trail of their makers, left no other trace.

Analysis of the child's DNA revealed that the boy's family members connected the Anzick boy to his widespread American relatives and to the Mal'ta boy who lived in Siberia about 12,000 years earlier. This evidence strongly suggests that Native American populations have a common Asian heritage as about 80 percent of native Central and South Americans were the direct descendants of the Mal'ta and Anzick boy family groups and, thus, are the true ancestors of Native Americans. For awhile, it was erroneously thought by some that European migrants (the Solutrians) had entered North America and had mixed their gene pool with those from Siberia.

During the next 1,000 years, or even in as short a time frame as several hundred years, this little band grew in size, not too much, but enough to consist of several dozen closely related families. As they traveled south, and east through what is now North America, they lived as true hunter/gatherers, but probably mostly as hunters as the variety of edible shrubs and herbs was limited at that time during that cold climate, although as the climate warmed significantly, more southerly plant species migrated northward. As these plant species grew in numbers and as individual plants, they were undoubtedly consumed by

15

the migrants. Perhaps some were noticed as having beneficial effects on health or well-being and this knowledge was passed on orally from generation to generation.

Concurrent with the arrival of these people into the New World, the European bison migrated with them. It was a much larger animal then, having a horn spread of over six feet. However, as this bison spread eastward, its size diminished somewhat as it adjusted to the changing climate and food availability and immense herds resulted. Bison later provided a rich source of food and materials for the descendants of these first human immigrants.

The first Americans, though, were never able to exterminate the bison as the bison reproduced faster than they could be killed by mere spears and associated weapons. It was not until the late 1800s that bison were nearly exterminated by single-shot Sharps and trap-door Springfield rifles in the hands of recently arrived European settlers. At one time only a dozen or so bison remained.

We now know that this band of hunter/gatherers passed through what is now the Yucatan Peninsula within the same 1,000-year time frame. The climate in Yucatan at that time was dry and as a 15- or 16-year-old girl was searching for water in a cave in the limestone terrain, she tumbled into a 90-foot-tall chamber, or *cenote*, breaking her pelvis. She died and her bones remained there for the next 12,000 years.

She had died among piles of bones of saber-toothed tigers, giant tapirs, and bears. The scientists who discovered her bones in 2007 named her Naia, after a water nymph of Greek mythology. Her mitochondrial DNA showed that she was directly related to the other early Americans who arrived across the Beringian land strait.

Another early group had passed through a site now known as *El Fin del Mundo* in Mexico's Sonora Desert and they also hunted with Clovis points. Bones from a gomphothere, a large, now extinct elephant-like mammal with two tusks extending from its lower jaw and two from its upper jaw, but smaller than mammoths and mastodons, were found at this site adjacent to four Clovis points.

A date from 13,400 years ago makes this site one of the oldest and southernmost Clovis sites known. This date and the finding of these Clovis points led some scientists to conjecture that Clovis points actually were developed in the Mexico area and then the technology moved rapidly northward.

The story of how the ancestors of what would eventually become the *González* family, in what is now Chile and Argentina, is the continuing object of this and the following chapter. Their migration had been swift and in only a few generations a part of this small band of intrepid explorers had migrated as far south to what is now known as *Monte Verde* in south-central Chile, and eventually even as far south as *Tierra del Fuego* on the southern tip of South America.

These early peoples undoubtedly conversed by some means and probably had a spoken language. Present-day evidence of a major language developed by these early people as they spread into South America was Amerind. As the Americas were populated, this basic language evolved into dozens of regional dialects. Today the major Andean dialect extends down the western coast of South America from present-day Ecuador to *Tierra del Fuego*, and consists of about 20 separate languages.

The Southern Andean portion that contains the **Mapudungún** (*"lengua de la tierra"* or "language of the earth") (=Araucanian) accounts for, along with the Aymara and Quechuan speakers in the northern Andes, over half of the entire Amerind population in both of the Americas.

As these native Americans, to be later to be generally known as the *mapuches* (which means *"gente de la tierra"* or "people of the earth"), spread into South America, they developed use of the *boleadoras* that allowed them to hunt large animals, including horses, that were abandoned by the Spaniards after some of their early explorations. Later the *mapuches* learned to use the horses for rapid mobility. These

17

early colonizers thrived in the Argentine pampas and after the arrival of the Spaniards, they were driven to the high altitude intermountain plateau that was rather isolated from both the east and west. The Spaniards called these people *"araucanos"* which means *"guerreros rebeldes"* or "rebel fighters." It was also a term used by the Incas in quechua.

This region was forested with Araucaria pine forests and it was upon the edible nuts produced by these trees that the sub-group that became known as the *Pehuenches* "**Pewenche**" (of the **Mapudungún**) thrived. They were people of the *pehuén* "**pewen**", or pine nut. The nuts were collected in great quantities and served as a reliable food base from which they learned to prepare a variety of foods and drinks. The pine nuts also had a great advantage in that they could be buried in the ground and would stay sound for months, thus allowing the *Pehuenches* to survive the long, cold winters in the region.

After conflicts with the Incas, the Spaniards, and the Chilean government, they concentrated in the *Lonquimay* region of present-day Chile but some also remained eastward in Argentina where at an earlier time they had occupied all the land from the Atlantic coast to the Pacific coast.

The long journey these people had made taught them a very important survival trait – that of family! Each member of the family had a value and, if the family acted as a group, they were better able to survive an inhospitable environment. That trait survives to this day in the modern *Pehuenches*. And it was during that long trek that they learned much about the medicinal values of certain plants!

The Clovis point
(redrawn from Sloan, 2005)

18

Chapter 3
Fleeing from European Colonialism
the 1800s

"Con certeza y con razón va cantando una canción, huinca, tregua, me robaron mi potrillo, mi ruca y el ternero." (With certainty and reason I go singing a song, a foreign devil stole my cart, my hut, and the heifer.) – Verse from song of *Mapuche* folklore.

These first Americans had quickly migrated southward into what is now South America, and then into southern Chile and Argentina. They led a harsh life during this migration. Hunger and injury were likely constant companions. However, after they had occupied the lands where they were to eventually stay, they led reasonably comfortable lives. But if their lives had been harsh up to this point, in one sense it was to eventually become much harsher after they clashed with European settlers.

These people had developed a complex language prior to their encounter with the Spaniards and certainly had developed a rich heritage during the past 10,000 plus years in the Americas. Unfortunately, they had been able to communicate and transfer knowledge down the generations only orally. It wasn't until after they met the first European settlers that they were able to adopt a written language, Spanish. So, most of what we know of their knowledge of medicinal plants stems from their collective knowledge starting from that time period.

At some point these native Americans were referred to by the Spaniards as Araucanians and this is the name by which they are generally known today. They were immortalized in the poem *"La Araucana"* by *Alonso de Ercilla*, an early Spanish explorer. But the term *Mapuche* is another name the natives have used to describe themselves. Both terms will be used somewhat interchangeably in this novel.

Pehuenche, conversely, is a more specialized sub-group that refers to those who settled in and now live in the inter-mountain plateau at the head of the *Lonquimay* Valley in Chile.

How the first native Americans came to be concentrated in the *Lonquimay* Valley is the result of incursions by the Incas prior to European settlement, which pushed these fiercely independent people southward and eastward, and then later westward during the nearly successful extermination of natives by the Argentine military in the 1800s and to some extent somewhat later by the Chilean military on the *Pehuenches* western range.

The Argentinian war of attrition against the *Pehuenches* was well underway by the time a young Charles Darwin visited southern Argentina in 1833. At that time, the wandering tribes were called horse Indians. They had adapted swiftly to the horse, abandoned by the retreating Spaniards after Argentinian independence in 1816. At first the horse was a source of food, but it soon gave them great mobility and allowed them to steal from and harass the outlying *estancias*. The warfare to exterminate them, though, was brutal and bloody, prompting Charles Darwin to observe that, "The warfare is too bloody to last."[1]

Darwin noted that it was sad to trace how attitudes toward the natives had changed. In 1535, when *Buenos Ayres* was founded, nearby villages of native Indians contained several thousand inhabitants. But, friction soon increased between them and their new Spanish neighbors until the Indians became more barbarous to match the intolerance of their new neighbors.

At the time of Charles Darwin, the government at *Buenos Ayres* had given command of the army to *General Juan Manuel de Rosas* and equipped it for the purpose of exterminating the Indians. The continual persecution soon changed the Indians from being farmers

---

[1] Darwin, Charles. A Naturalist's Voyage Round the World: The Voyage of The Beagle. Project Gutenberg EBook #3704 produced by Sue Asscher, August 6, 2008. The e-version is based on the 1890 11ᵗʰ edition. (The book first appeared in 1839.)

living in villages to wandering the open plains without a home. They naturally tried to defend themselves.

Extermination continued during the 1800s until the 1870s when *General Julio Argentino Roca* extended Argentine power into the Patagonian desert and ended the possibility of Chilean expansion there. A decisive event had occurred in 1872 when the Indian leader *Calfucura* and 6,000 followers attacked several cities, killing 300 settlers and driving off 200,000 head of cattle. These they drove to Chile, where they were welcomed, and they traded the cattle for goods. As early as 1830, Chilean invaders had begun to settle in Patagonia with the intention of laying claim to those lands for Chile. As the war of extermination continued, Chile initially supported the natives because they hoped to wrest those lands from the Argentinians.

In 1875, *Adolfo Alsina*, the Argentinian Minister of War, decisively attacked the Indians and forced them to retreat. He then constructed a 233 mile trench that served as a barrier to the unconquered territories to the west. It was ten feet wide and eight feet deep and mainly served as an obstacle to cattle drives by the Indians.

Late in 1878, *General Roca* believed that the only solution to the Indian problem was to finally exterminate the Indians. He started a sweep of the area between the *Alsina* trench and the *Negro* River. After numerous hostile encounters, thousands of Indians were either killed or captured. Large numbers of surviving Indians migrated far westward into the zone around *Cuarrehue* and *Pucón*, Chile.

The Spaniards and the *Mapuches* achieved an uneasy truce, with the Spaniards unable to vanquish the *Mapuches*, and the latter barely able to defend their homeland. In a meeting between the two adversaries in 1641, both sides compromised and a treaty was signed giving the *Mapuches* title to all the lands south of the *Biobío* River. After 1817, however, when Chile won its independence from Spain, the truce was broken as new settlers contested ownership of the lands. The Chilean government's official program of pacification began in 1861 and, by 1883, the lands were declared pacified. This period was a long process

21

of military occupation as the Chilean government constructed a series of forts across southern Chile, from the coast to the Andean *Cordillera*. A last fort was built at the village of *Lonquimay* and the area was opened up to European settlement. Like their ancestors in North America, the *Mapuches* were duped with treaty promises and handshakes.

The first wave of European immigrants arrived between 1883 and 1884, reaching the northern part of the area. They came with the promise of a great economic future. To some extent, they were also duped by the economic incentive. Five hundred families of Spanish, French, Swiss, and German origin were among the first arrivals. At the beginning of the 20th century, colonists from The Netherlands and Italy also arrived. At the end of the 19th century the government constructed a number of railroad lines to tie the region together. The first rail-line united *Victoria* with *Temuco*, and later with *Curacautín*, and then with *Malalcahuello*, and finally with *Lonquimay* via the tunnel at *Las Raíces*.

Arrival of the railroad marked the beginning of forest exploitation in the zone and, for a period of only forty years, much of the formerly vast expanses of Araucaria forests were lost to the sawmill and uncontrolled fires. Many of these forests were hundreds to thousands of years old and would be almost impossible to replace.

Sometime before the arrival of Europeans in this part of South America, after most of the big game was long gone, including the giant ground sloths, the *Mapuches* began a shift in their diet to include the domesticated *guanaco* and smaller wild animals such as rabbits and birds. After the introduction of Spanish animals, they also ate cows, sheep, horses, and pigs. As European colonization encroached on their territory they were forced to shift to do less hunting and more cultivation of such plants as potatoes, corn and other native plants including beans, cloves, and *quinoa*. They also collected fruits of *copihue*, *boldo*, *peumo*, *maqui*, *luma*, and *cocos* of the Chilean palm. They collected wild honey. Excavations at the *Monte Verde* site in southern Chile found potatoes (a 13,000-year-old specimen of *Solanum maglia*, a wild potato species).

Subsistence farming forced them to move closer together into cooperative family units to share work, trade, and defense and they tightened their grip on their land. This closeness to the land forced them to develop an intimate knowledge of the various plant species and whatever edible or other beneficial value they might have. Their survival and well-being depended on it. And they did this pretty much on their own, except for some contact with their neighboring families. As they mutually explored their environment, they had to test every plant to see what value it might have for them. Nutritional value was relatively easy to determine, testing for beneficial effects on health was quite another task, which took millennia to perfect.

By not spreading themselves too thinly they were able to resist domination by the Incas and the later attempted extermination by the Spaniards. They might have preferred to live mainly in the climatically more agreeable Central Valley of Chile but when the Incas began their conquest southward from what is now Peru, the small group of families decided to migrate up into the *Andes* mountains and over into what is now Argentina to escape the Incas' raids, yet still survive with an initially meager source of food.

They developed an almost symbiotic relationship with the native Araucaria pines that were abundant in the valley. An Araucaria pine, when mature, is a large tree with a single, straight, and usually branchless trunk topped by an umbrella-like crown of downwardly hanging curved branches. The female trees produce cones with large nuts that are quite nutritious and were a valued food to the *Pehuenches*. At the time of human arrival in the valley, vast Araucaria pine forests covered most of the region, from Argentina to the Chilean coast. By adjusting to this treasure house of pine forest they were able not only to survive a dramatic change in diet, but, in fact, actually thrived by collecting large amounts of the nutritious pine nuts ensuring plenty of food for consumption in the winter season. Just prior to European contact, the *Pehuenches* lived a harsh life but were able to produce all their own food and clothing. This trait allowed them to more or less survive the first onslaughts of European invasion.

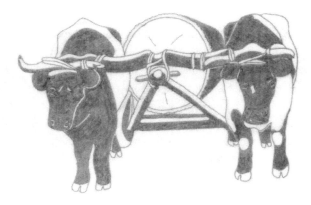

Yoke of oxen, transporting an Araucaria pine log.

Chapter 4
Into the Modern Era
1920

"Pucha que es linda mi tierra." (Gosh, my country is beautiful!)
– Verse of music from Chilean folklore.

Robert might have never heard of this group of Native Americans if it had not been for a Frenchman who arrived in the valley in 1920. Young Jean Piñon Retif was a recent veteran of the Great War in Europe. He had somehow survived four years of brutal war and was so disenchanted with life in Europe that he decided to go as far away from civilization as he could.

He was typical of many Americans at that time whom had also been disenfranchised by the war. Today we might say that he had a form of post-traumatic stress disorder. Instead of turning to a life of alcohol he decided to do something with his life and go far away. He had distant family members living in *Talca*, Chile who had migrated there to work in the vineyards and so he decided to go there for a visit.

At that time, memories of many Chileans still had a strong connection with the earlier frontier life and it was easy to strike up a conversation with strangers regarding memories from their past. Soon after Jean arrived in Chile, he became enchanted with the stories of the Araucanian natives who lived in the south and were never subjugated by the Incas or the Spanish or the Chilean government. He was impressed by how they had surmounted their hardships and so, he decided to visit some of these people and get to know them on his way to Argentina.

Jean planned to make a trek from the frontier town of *Temuco*, right on the border of the old frontier where a lot of Germans had subsequently settled, and go up into the interior of Chile toward Argentina. He didn't want to stay long in *Temuco* as he had just had enough dealings with the Germans in the war. He thought he might like to eventually settle in southern Argentina and buy a ranch in the *pampas* where not many people lived and he could isolate himself from humanity's cruelty to humanity.

He took the train from *Santiago* to *Talca* and then to *Temuco* where he purchased two horses to begin the trek up the *Lonquimay* Valley toward Argentina. Although motorcars were just beginning to become common in the area, he felt that horses might be a more reliable form of transportation. He was told that the roads were not very passable for motorized vehicles. After several weeks of moving from village to village along the *Cautín* River he finally arrived at *Curacautín*. After resting there for several days, he purchased more supplies and continued his trek up the valley. The only road to *Lonquimay*, the next village, if it could be called that, was over the "*Camino Las Raíces*", a seasonal road over the *cordillera* and through the heart of several extensive Araucaria pine forests.

Lonquimay was less than 62 miles away and he thought that a leisurely ride would help to clear his head of recurring memories of the agonies he had suffered in the recent war. As he rode along, and camped wherever he wished, he marveled at the majestic Araucaria pine forests he passed through. And the sky was such an intense cornflower blue that it seemed to pull at his eyes as if it were magnetic whenever he glanced at it. He was actually beginning to like this valley as there were few people living there and the solitude felt wonderful.

Jean stopped and talked with *Pehuenches* herding their cattle and sheep along the way, moving them into the fresh grazing in the high country. He learned that outside interests were threatening inroads into the *Lonquimay* Valley. An outsider, a white cattle rancher, had settled in the valley and was now claiming ownership of most of the land along

26

the *Biobío* River to the east of *Lonquimay*. He was so sure of his claim that in that same year he had begun negotiating with a sawmill owner to log some of the Araucaria pine forests, claiming them as his own. The *Pehuenches* began to resist but had little hope of proving their ownership of the land to the government in *Santiago*. At that time, Araucanian natives were considered second-class citizens by many Chileans and prejudiced against, much as the Negroes were in the United States.

Jean had just traveled down out of the mountains and was back into the *Lonquimay* Valley. He could see scattered houses ahead and suspected he was getting close to the town of *Lonquimay*. He thought he would camp one more night before entering town and as he was preparing camp late that afternoon along the *Naranjo* River, he thought he heard someone arguing in a loud voice. The argument quickly rose *in crescendo* and then was punctuated by screams. He thought they were of a woman!

Jean ran in the direction of the screams. As he came around a bend in the river he saw three men who appeared to be assaulting a young woman. As her screams increased, he grabbed a large stick from the ground and charged the group. Jean was not afraid, he had faced far worse in the trenches of the Somme. When the men saw him, one pulled a small pistol from his pocket and aimed it at Jean. Jean hit the man's arm and the pistol went flying. Jean hit another man over the shoulder and the third alongside his head, each time with a crunch as the stick broke off leaving a shorter piece.

Jean thought it was quite a sight and chuckled as he watched the three men run away, with all three missing their pants and shoes. Jean then turned toward the sobbing and partially naked girl. She came toward him and melted in his arms as she sobbed even more forcefully. Being the gentleman that he was, he immediately removed his coat and placed it around her shoulders.

"What is your name?" he queried in French, and then again in his broken Spanish as he realized she probably didn't understand French. "*Luisa*," she whispered between sobs. "Who were those men?" he asked. *"No sé pero creo que trabajan en el aserradero nuevo. Son extranjeros, como usted,"* (I don't know who they are, but I think they work in the new sawmill. They are foreigners, like you.) she replied, and then realized that she was in his arms and drew away.

Jean realized that she was probably almost as afraid of him as she was of those men. "Do you live near here? Let me take you home." *"Gracias,"* she said. "I was down here picking some herbs for my sick father. I live just down the valley along the river." So, Jean led her back to his campsite, helped her mount his horse, and then he walked beside the horse as they went to her home.

When they entered the yard and a dog began barking, Jean was afraid that he would be blamed for her disheveled condition, but as soon as her mother came out, *Luisa* assured her that this strange man had, in fact, probably saved her from a certain rape, and perhaps, had even saved her life. By this time several neighbors had shown up and surrounded the trio, at first in a rather hostile manner that quickly changed into treating him as a hero. Each time a new neighbor joined the group, the story was retold, and Jean began to relax a little.

Luisa's mother could not do enough for him. He was offered numerous drinks of *chicha* and soon was barely able to stand. *Luisa* took him in to see her sick father. The man sat up in the bed and looked deep into Jean's eyes as *Luisa* related what had happened to her. He extended his hand and grasped Jean's with a firm grip and Jean knew the man was deeply grateful for what he had done.

Then, as Jean prepared to leave, *Luisa's* parents insisted that he remain there for a few days as their guest. So, Jean spent the next few days getting to know the family and *Luisa*, and perhaps it was no surprise that he agreed to stay there a while longer.

Later that summer, Jean Piñon Retiff and *Luisa Melinir* were married in the little church in *Lonquimay*. Jean didn't know what he would do for a living but he helped the family with their livestock and expanded garden. In the fall he helped harvest very large amounts of *pehuenes*, which they sold for cash, and they passed that first winter very well. As they passed one of the first cold winter evenings sitting by the stove and discussing just about everything, Jean felt very contented with his life and he somehow knew that he would never make it to the Argentine *pampas*.

In the following spring, Jean and *Luisa* traveled to *Talca* and stayed several days at a house at *3y4 Sur Poniente 818,* where Jean had relatives. They then took the train to *Santiago,* to *2266 San Alfonso,* very close to the *Estación Central,* where some of *Luisa's* relatives lived, and Jean made arrangements with his family in France to send some money from his mother's estate and some of her extra furniture to Chile. The money and furniture came within a few months and he and *Luisa* planned the construction of their new house.

The site for their new house was on land Jean had purchased from *Luisa's* father and was located several miles or so up the *Naranjo* River, near to the intersection of the *Río Naranjo* with the *Biobío* River. The location was at the mouth of a little valley, which would provide shelter from the heavy winter snows. The house site was bordered on the south by a series of small ranges and the *Lonquimay* Valley on the north. The entry road was adjacent to a small stream and the area was fairly isolated yet within walking distance of the village of *Lonquimay.*

Their house was completely unorthodox for the area and it was patterned after the style then common in the Swiss Alps. It had a steep roof with a wide overhang to help withstand the heavy snows that occasionally occurred in the valley. The roof and exterior walls were shingled with *alerce* tiles. The interior walls were covered with vertical boards of *ciprés de la cordillera,* sawn from logs harvested on forestland Jean had purchased from *Luisa's* parents. Some boards were nearly a foot wide. The frame construction walls were filled with dry sawdust, providing much needed insulation against the cold winter months. The house had indoor plumbing with an inside bathroom, kitchen, and all the latest amenities then common in France among the upper class.

The front of the house faced the river and had large glass windows that Jean had to have brought down from *Santiago.* The entry road turned off the public road, crossed a bridge over a small stream, and then curved around to the east side of the house and then around to the back where the main entrance was located. Several outbuildings and a large barn comprised the little farm site.

The story of Jean and *Luisa* became a legend in the valley. *Luisa* became a respected **machi** (shaman) and she and Jean were loved and respected by all. Their daughter, *Claudia*, continued work that her father had begun to protect the interests of the *Pehuenches* as land grabbing and logging interests became more powerful. Jean eventually became the community **lonco**, an elder responsible for administering community affairs and gatherings. He was instrumental in helping the valley residents to form cooperatives to sell sheep, cattle, and handicrafts. Although life was always harsh there, the formation of cooperatives led to somewhat better economic conditions for many of the valley's residents.

Claudia married *Juan González*, another *Pehuenche* but with some Spanish blood in his veins, and they had two children, a son, *Miguel*, and a daughter, *Rosa*. It is with the family of *Juan* and *Claudia* that our story continues in more detail.

Luisa Melinir, when she was 8 years old, had a dream that she was going to be a **machi.** Her grandmother had been a **machi** also, but *Luisa's* mother had not had the calling, or gift, if one wanted to think of it in that way. *Luisa's* daughter, *Claudia*, had been trained by her great grandmother to be a **machi** but had never pursued it when she was a young woman. She had met *Juan González* and they spent several years collecting and researching folklore music. After *Juan* and *Claudia* became very successful as folk singers, *Claudia* returned to her training as a **machi**, but rather than becoming a practicing **machi** who diagnosed patients and prescribed medical treatments, she and *Juan* became dedicated to seeking and recording for the sake of posterity, plants and whatever medicinal remedies or benefits those plants might have. At the time that Robert first visited them, they had spent about ten years in that endeavor and had built quite a reputation in Chile and

30

Argentina, and even around the world. They also had a large garden and greenhouse where they propagated many medicinal plants.

The house that Jean and *Luisa* built, and where *Juan* and *Claudia* later lived.

Chapter 5
Upper Kintla Lake,
Glacier National Park, Montana
July 1962

"This is no shit." – Usually the first sentence in any story about
smoke jumpers.

Robert awoke instantly when the pilot of the DC-2 throttled
back and entered the slow see-saw motion of the plane as the pilot and
spotter took the first look-see over the fire. Robert had been sitting in
a cramped position for over an hour now and was beginning to feel
drowsy. He had taken off his helmet as soon as the plane cleared the
runway but that did not offer much relief. The harness, which was
comparatively loose an hour ago, was now digging into his shoulders
and the strap across his chest prevented him from taking little more
than short, shallow breaths.

Added to that discomfort was the weight of the 24-foot-
diameter emergency parachute on his chest and the cramped harness of
the 32-foot-diameter main chute on his back, plus being dressed in an
insulated nylon jump suit. The jump suit also had a 12-inch collar that
prevented much air circulation around one's head, so within a few
minutes of take off, he was sitting in a pocket of sleep-inducing carbon
dioxide. He lay on his parachute and tried to tell himself that he was
comfortable, but he wasn't. The plane was rolling from side to side and
he began to feel sick.

The pilot and the spotter began an animated conversation over
their radio headsets about the safest place to drop the jumpers and their
equipment and the best approach to that site. With that information in
mind the pilot throttled up slightly as he swung the plane over to the

left and then began to fly back around as he decided the best angle at which to fly over the fire and approach the jump spot.

As the pilot was preparing for the first set of jumpers to leave the plane, Robert tried to keep from being sick by recalling his first day of the four-week training period at the Missoula Smokejumper Base with the other 56 trainees. The training period was rigorous to say the least, but it was also fun and very interesting. Each morning at 5:30 the trainees had to report out on the landing apron in front of the parachute loft for a half-hour of calisthenics.

After breakfast, approximately half of the day was spent in the classroom learning fire behavior, fire control techniques, first aid, and the theory of safe parachuting. The rest of the day was spent either out in the woods felling snags, building fire lines, climbing trees with the spurs, or working out on the dreaded training units.

The units were designed to make the training so rigorous and monotonous that each jumper would behave instinctively, without taking time to think about what to do. It was much like military training. In fact, at the beginning of World War II, the military officers of the fledging airborne division of the U. S. Army came to Missoula to observe how the smokejumpers trained.

One of the units was a shock tower designed to acquaint trainees with the opening shock of a parachute as it unraveled from the backboard on the jumper's back. The trainees started jumping off at the 16-foot level to get the feel of jumping into thin air and, after one or two jumps, graduated to the 32-foot level. The Canadian swing and "A" frames were used to teach trainees the proper way to perform the Allen roll when landing in order to prevent sprained ankles or a concussion.

The instructors tried to pound the training into the trainee's heads and if they saw a sloppy roll the trainee was required to do 25 pushups in his complete jump suit. Robert recalled spending a good share of his time doing pushups and it wasn't unusual for a trainee to do several hundred a day as punishment for some training infraction.

Since a smokejumper sometimes lands in a tree, another of the units was designed to train a jumper how to get out of a tree without breaking his neck. A 100-foot-long nylon webbing called a let-down rope was used for this purpose and was carried in a pocket on the left leg. After landing in a tree, the jumper was to secure one end of the let-down rope to his harness and then, after slipping out of his harness, slide down the rope to the ground. With practice the complete let down should take less than two minutes.

During the third and fourth weeks the trainees made their seven practice jumps, jumping out of a variety of airplanes. The tiny Travelaire, and later the Twin Beechcraft, were used to carry two or three jumpers to a small fire and the former was one of the first airplanes used for smokejumping. Later the larger Ford Trimotor was a mainstay on both large and small fires. Its slow speed and extreme maneuverability made it perfect for flying in the mountainous terrain where most forest fires occurred. Faster DC-2s and DC-3s were widely used somewhat later, as was the much larger C-46, especially for big fires.

Robert didn't particularly like jumping out of the C-46. It was a big plane by smokejumper standards, and its glide speed for jumping was a little too fast for him. You had to throw yourself out the door in order to safely enter the slip-stream of air rushing by the open door and then when the parachute opened, the shock was so great that you felt as if you were going to be turned inside out. There was really no danger, of course, but it still was a rough opening, especially with the 32' diameter parachutes being used more and more now.

His favorite planes were the DC-2s, with the DC-3s being a close second. He had always wanted to jump out of one of the Ford Trimotors but had never had the opportunity. He knew it would be his favorite because it had real class and a long history of use in firefighting.

The smaller Twin Beechcraft was okay but he felt nervous flying in a plane that stayed aloft and flew mainly through the power of its two large engines. He had seen the wreckage of one of these planes that crashed at the Missoula airport on takeoff when one of its engines failed. It dropped and veered to the side so suddenly that the pilot never had a chance to react.

The other feature he didn't like about the C-46 was that the door was so wide. You couldn't reach both edges when exiting the plane to help throw yourself out the door, and that concern came back to haunt him on what would later turn out to be his last fire jump.

Today, though, as the pilot maneuvered the DC-2 around the mountain and entered the glide path in preparation for the first stick of jumpers, in what was to be Robert's next to last fire jump, Robert recalled his first fire jump last year. It seemed like a long time ago now, after all that had happened to him, especially the offer of the assistantship. But he could still visualize everything about that jump.

Suddenly, above the deep, bumblebee in-and-out synchronous roar and vibration of the two powerful engines and the shrill scream of the slipstream past the open door, he heard his name called. He looked toward the rear of the plane and saw the spotter motioning to him. They were at the fire now and he was to jump in the first stick.

After some difficulty, he got to his feet and hobbled to the rear of the plane. Since this was a DC-2, only two men could jump at a time. In the DC-3, three men can jump in a stick because the fuselage is a little wider. The foreman was first and Robert would follow. The spotter helped hook up the static lines to the cable that is bolted across the rear bulkhead and made a final check of all the harnesses and buckles.

Then, as the roar of engines quieted down and became smoother as the pilot throttled back, Robert knew that the plane was entering the glide path. He stepped close behind the foreman with his right foot forward so that when he took one more step toward the door, he would step past the threshold and out into the slipstream which would catch his right leg as it left the doorway and turn him facing toward the rear of the plane.

Robert looked through the door opening and there, only a little over a thousand feet below, was some of the most rugged country in the Inland Empire, and very dangerous to jump into. It is covered with a shaggy green carpet of trees and scattered here and there were tall, rotten snags and rocky outcroppings.

The spotter yelled, "There is a 2-mile-an hour breeze blowing up the canyon so it will be tricky. There aren't any openings so you will have to tree-up. Keep headed into the wind all the way down." The spotter then snapped his goggles over his eyes and jumped down to the floor. For what seemed like an eternity but was actually only 5 or 7 seconds he lay there motionless with his head half out the door sighting on the jump spot.

When the plane was directly over the jump spot he very deliberately rolled back out of the doorway and then with a "Go get 'um Tiger!" he slapped the foreman on the back of his left leg. The foreman disappeared through the doorway; Robert crouched down and took one step forward and threw himself after him with his right leg leaving the plane first.

This fire, which only involved half a dozen jumpers, was a jumper's dream. It had adequate manpower to control, was not too large to begin with, and the weather cooperated to make it almost a joy to fight. It was easily controlled the first day, and then after several more days mopping up, the jumpers hiked out to the nearest ranger station where they were fed and then loaded onto a bus for the ride back to the smokejumper base in Missoula. As he was sitting on the bus, Robert thought about his life thus far and the momentous changes that the end of this fire season would bring to his life.

Robert loved smokejumping but knew that this would be his last summer for jumping. It had been a slow fire season so far and he was having trouble saving enough money from overtime firefighting to fund his graduate studies at Montana State University for the next school year. It wasn't like that last year, in 1961, the summer of the Sleeping Child Fire in Idaho. Then, there weren't enough

36

smokejumpers, or even ground pounders, to handle the number of fires burning at any one time in the Inland Empire. He racked up a lot of overtime for his studies that year and still had a little left for the next year.

Also, the excitement and lure of firefighting was fading somewhat and, although he didn't fully realize it yet, he was developing a real interest in medicinal plants useful as health remedies. Then he met several Peace Corps Volunteers recently returned from Chile and Peru who were now studying at the then Montana State University in Missoula. He visited with them and they tried to answer his many questions about life there.

If all went according to plan, he would graduate a year later, in late spring, from the Dept. of Botany and had already been offered a research assistant position in the Department. The condition was that he be willing to go to Chile, in South America, to study and collect medicinal plants and herbal remedies of the indigenous natives. Robert would have been happy to go anywhere in South America.

The Department had been the recipient of an NIH grant to study medicinal plants in various countries in South America. The study in Chile was to be a pilot study to determine the efficacy of this approach and develop the methodology to be used in future studies. Other graduate students at the University in Missoula and at other universities around the United States would follow-up on the material Robert was to collect and extract chemicals and determine their effectiveness in laboratory studies.

After he was offered the assistantship, he studied historical accounts of Spanish expeditions in Mexico, Peru, Venezuela, and Chile. After reading Prescott's classic account of the War of the Pacific, he began to feel a kinship with the people, the land, and the plants and forests that grew there. Through interlibrary loan he borrowed major first accounts by La Condamine, Bonpland, Von Humboldt, and other great plant explorers, and re-lived their experiences in being the first to discover and describe the exotic plant life of South America.

The plant life in Chile was especially interesting because it had evolved in isolation from the other major geographic areas of South America and had a closer affinity to the present vegetation of New Zealand, showing that those plants had co-evolved dating back to before the major split-up of the previous continental landform.

A week after he returned to Missoula he was back at the top of the jump list, and so it was no surprise when he was called early one Monday morning to prepare for a flight to the northwestern corner of Glacier National Park. Soon the C-46 was loading jumpers for the several hour flight. As the plane approached its destination, the tired, and bored, jumpers began to get to their feet and stretch as best as they could encumbered with two parachutes, a personal gear bag, a let-down rope, and compressed into a restraining white nylon jumpsuit.

Robert, too, got up and began checking his neighbor's gear and bouncing around on the floor as the plane settled into the first jump glide path. The spotter had already thrown out the markers on the previous pass and was mentally calculating the drift that the first stick of jumpers would experience. In a DC-2, a stick usually consisted of 2 jumpers, both exiting the plane one after the other. In the larger DC-3s or C-46s, 3-man sticks were the norm. This was going to be a big fire and this C-46 was getting ready to drop jumpers, and a DC-3 had just taken off from the Missoula airport with another load of jumpers. These two planes were especially useful on larger fires when as many as 44 men, or even more, would jump on what would become known as a project fire.

Robert, though, preferred the smaller, 2, 3, or 4 man fires. Small fires could usually be suppressed with only a few fire fighters and the whole operation was usually more relaxed. Sometimes, though, small fires blew up unexpectedly and reinforcements were necessary. This might involve dropping more jumpers or dropping a load or two of flame retardant.

Dropping more jumpers was usually an embarrassment to the men already on the fire, but sometimes things happened such as a change in wind direction or velocity that could completely and quickly change the fire-behavior situation. Part of that, though, was the shot of adrenaline, which was probably the major reason why young men, and years later young women, became smokejumpers.

Today, though, this fire, which became known as the Upper Kintla Lake Fire, was the kind of fire Robert didn't particularly like. It was a project fire. The first sets of jumps consisted of 44 jumpers. Later, that number would be increased, mainly because the fire was spreading fast, but also partially because it was an otherwise slow fire season and the jump base could be a little extravagant with the number of jumpers sent to any particular fire. More jumpers, however, meant more confusion and an increased chance of accidents.

The flight path over the jump spot was rather circuitous because the jump spot was in a long narrow valley surrounded by tall mountains and carpeted with huckleberry bushes. So, the plane had to fly around a mountain each time after a stick of jumpers left the plane. Normally jumpers exit the plane at about 1000 feet above the ground. This is high enough to allow the jumper to steer for the jump spot, or adjust for occasional malfunctions of the parachute, or deploy the reserve chute if all else fails. Today, though, jumpers were exiting at about over 3,000 ft. elevation. More chance of an accident, but today, for Robert, it would turn out to be to his benefit.

Robert was about halfway back in the cluster of jumpers and equipment. As the first jumpers began exiting the plane, the remaining jumpers stood and began checking their own and each other's gear for the last time. The flight from Missoula to Glacier Park had taken about 2 ½ hours and was rather bumpy in the early morning flight. Several jumpers were feeling a little airsick and would be glad to exit the plane.

Back toward the tail end of the fuselage was a young man who had been partying the night before. He was the last man to board the plane and was almost left at the airport because he arrived just as the plane was leaving. At any rate, the poor kid was sitting on the floor and looking worse and worse with each bump of the plane. After about an hour he upchucked what seemed like gallons of pure green bile.

Fortunately, after a trickle of bile reached the front end of the aircraft, the spotter saw it and grabbed an elongated cardboard box containing climbing spurs and tossed it to the sick jumper. The remaining bile, and it seemed like there was still a lot of it, went in there. He wondered who would be the unfortunate individual who had to use those climbing spurs. It would be a good reason to avoid treeing up on this fire.

Unfortunately, the rivulet of green bile that had worked its way forward from the tail end of the plane turned out to be pretty slippery. When Robert's turn to jump came, he found he was the second man in a three-man-stick. There was nothing to hang onto except each other as he and the other two jumpers slipped and slid around each time the plane dropped or rose a few feet with the turbulence.

Robert held himself in place mainly by will power. When the spotter slapped the lead man's leg as the signal to jump, he and the other two jumpers slid out the door as a three-man mass of humanity with gobs of green goo dripping from their boots.

As the three men exited the plane's door and began to fall, Robert observed the man in front of him and his parachute as it began to unwrap from its backboard. As if in slow motion, he distinctly saw a cluster of shroud lines unfold and realized that he was falling between several of them.

Thankfully, both parachutes fully opened with double jolts, but as they were unfolding, he found that he was entangled among those lines. With his back to the jumper he was entangled with he really couldn't do much because he couldn't see what was happening. But, fortunately, the other jumper had a good line of sight and told him which lines to pull down and then roll over in order to free himself from the entangling mess and then roll free.

As he began to extricate himself from the tangle of shroud lines he had to chuckle as he recalled the words of the jumper as he was commanding him what to do, "Robert, you son-of-a–bitch, don't you dare cut any of my lines!" With that thought, he rolled out of the last lines, swung once, and then stepped out on the ground and onto a nice, soft huckleberry bush. He didn't even have to do an Allen roll when he landed. If they had not had the extra 2,000 feet of jump time a sprained ankle, or worse, could have been the result.

Robert made only a few more jumps that summer, but no fire jumps. The fall rains started early and the forest fuels were too wet to ignite from lightning strikes. The few jumps he made were to remote peaks to clear off the trees and to convert those mountaintops for use as helicopter landing pads. This was his last fire jump but his smokejumping experience had prepared him well for what the future was to bring. The main thing he would miss would be the adrenaline rush when exiting from the open door of an airplane. He had begun his graduate studies with a passion and was ready to face the future! His experiences as a smokejumper taught him that when faced with danger, one must quickly assess the situation then act decisively.

A Douglas DC-2 aircraft on a firefighting mission.
Two smokejumpers have exited the plane and their
parachutes have just begun to deploy.

Chapter 6
The Medicinal Plant Collector
1970

"El Yerbatero" (The medicinal plant doctor.) – Title of song from
Chilean folklore.

What started as a small business that Robert was associated
with had an interesting conception and proves that even nerds can
become successful in business. The initiation of Pharmtec began when
a half-dozen upper class students at the then Montana State University
in Missoula met during a drinking party at the beginning of their junior
year at the university. It was a strange group - they had a common love
for botany, not partying! As the group went through each year of their
studies, there were seldom more than two or three students in the
group during any given year but this year the group consisted of five
dedicated young men and one young woman who all shared an almost
religious interest in botany. Two of the five young men were foresters.

The common thread between all of them was their love for
plants of all kinds, from the mightiest trees down to the lowliest herbs.
One discussion after another during their senior year led to a sort of
camaraderie as they collectively reflected on how they might make a
living with their knowledge and love of plants. At that time, two
decades after the Second World War, the economy was still booming
and the forestry majors could easily find work with the USDA Forest
Service, the BLM, or with any of a variety of state forestry
organizations. The botany majors had fewer employment possibilities,
as there were few jobs except for teaching in high school science
programs, none of which paid more than a bare living wage.

One of Robert's forestry friends, Dick Babcock, had an idea –
suppose they started a company that sold medicinal plants as remedies

for human ailments. Robert had a small estate from his grandfather that he was willing to invest and Dick had relatively wealthy parents who might be willing to assist them in getting started. If they collected and dried medicinal plants, perhaps they could package them and sell the product to consumers interested in using such remedies. All the students had some knowledge of some such remedies that their parents and grandparents had exposed them to when they were children.

The group discussed the difficulties, and possibilities, and agreed to join in the formation of the fledging company, initially on a part-time basis and then later full-time if the finances of the business would allow it. One of the partners lived in Hamilton, Montana and his retiring grandfather owned a family medical laboratory that he would let the group use for free in order to help get them started. Robert had been born and raised in Missoula, and his parents were happy for him to live with them at no cost, at least until the venture became economically successful. None of the original group could know at that time just how successful their venture was to become. By their good fortune, they were on the cusp of a major revolution in human health care.

During his last years at Missoula, and especially in graduate school, Robert studied Spanish and took as many elective courses in chemistry as he could. Several friends, including Dick, graduated two years ahead of him and began to assemble the fledgling company. They purchased some common dried plants with known remedies and began to process, package, and sell them. Their success was rather immediate and surprising, and the company soon gained a national following.

Robert felt, though, that their best business opportunity would be to handle medicinal plants that had a long history of human use, acceptance and, therefore, a long history of efficacy. His readings about the plant explorations in South America convinced him that business success lay in that direction. The tropical, or at least temperate, climate during human migration there had guaranteed a large variety of plant species to study.

So, the group collectively chose Chile as the object of their exploratory work. It was a long, narrow country with a good road system and one person could probably do a thorough survey of the complete country. *Muñoz's* book on the identification of Chilean flora had just been published and Robert would be able to verify identifications of plants he collected. So, on that scary October day following graduation, he purchased a Panagra air ticket to *Santiago*, Chile, and loaded with plant presses and a USDA Plant Quarantine Permit to send seeds and dried plant parts into the United States, he left for Chile.

Robert planned his survey for native Chilean plants with herbal remedies by visiting with country folk he encountered along his meanders in the Central Valley of Chile. He left *Santiago* and drove straight South to *Puerto Montt* where he began a northward trek of exploration, planning to eventually finish his work in *La Serena*. His strategy seemed rather naïve - he would visit the open-air markets and see what kind of herbal remedies were for sale there. He would ask questions about what benefit they might have and anything he could learn about them.

Although he decided to first concentrate his quest in the area north of *Puerto Montt*, he realized that eventually he would also have to explore the less-populated country south of *Puerto Montt*. When he questioned local medicinal plant vendors they often gave him names of local producers and collectors so he had a foot in the door when he sought them out. After he started, he wished he had studied Spanish a little more. But, he had a strong desire to learn and he soon did very well.

Before leaving the States he had scoured all the interlibrary loan literature he could find on Chilean plant and herbal remedies so he had a good head start on the project. Now he would have to actually identify and collect plant samples and send seeds and tissue samples back to the States.

He actually started his explorations in the *Puerto Montt* region by visiting with members of a native aboriginal tribe known as the *Cuncos*. At first, tribe members were reluctant to speak with him but, as he persisted with his questions, they recognized that he was serious in his goal of learning about the native plants and the remedies associated with them.

During the next two summers of explorations he met with representatives of the *Huilliches* and later with the *Mapuches*. He had not yet sought out the *Poyas* and *Puelches* since these were located on the east side of the *Andes* in Argentina and they were relatively inaccessible from the Chilean side. His plan was to eventually go north to the *Lonquimay* Valley, meet with the *Pehuenche* natives living there, and when that work was finished, cross over into Argentina and return southward on the Argentine side of the *Andes* to meet with members of the latter two tribes.

He had noted that there was a common unity of many plants recognized as having remedial properties, so in some ways his work became a little easier with each trip. All of these tribes were part of the larger Araucanian race, not vanquished by either the Incas or by the Spanish or by the Chilean government after Chile's independence from Spain.

The indigenous history of the usefulness of herbal remedies was well known when the Spaniards arrived. During the 14,000, or so, years after they arrived in the *pampas*, these peoples had experienced centuries of trial and error in discovering the efficacious benefits of certain plants. In other words, many of these remedies worked, and some worked very well.

The purpose of Robert's surveys was to collect as much information as possible about medicinal plants and the health benefits they provided and, where possible, collect the actual plant tissues and also seeds. He had a Plant Import Certificate from the USDA that allowed him to ship a wide range of plant materials to the Pharmtec laboratory in Hamilton, Montana. After their initial analyses, the

45

scientists could request additional materials on which to conduct further tests.

When the NIH grant, which funded their early work, was terminated due to budget-cutting by Congress in order to fund the war in Vietnam, and they could no longer realistically continue significant extraction and expensive testing research, their focus shifted to identifying medicinal plants, growing them in the greenhouse, harvesting, packaging, and then marketing the product. When this shift in focus occurred, Robert's work in Chile became particularly important. He had to know for sure which plants were responsible for alleviating specific ailments.

Robert's new and somewhat shortened responsibility was to survey the southern part of Chile roughly from *Temuco* southward to *Puerto Montt*. If that work produced positive results, he would then expand his surveys to include the areas north of *Temuco*, and south of *Puerto Montt*. Long-range research planning included extending the surveys to Argentina, and then, perhaps, to other South American countries.

As Robert identified plants associated with medicinal traits, he would then visit the *Museo de Historia Natural* in *Santiago* and examine the herbaria there and piece together range maps of these herbal plants. After he began his work, he found that personnel at this museum had a lot of information that they were eager to share with him. Chilean scientists had a lot of interest in doing exactly what Robert was doing but they lacked financial backing to pursue their interests. A great help to Robert was the recently published *"Sinopsis de la Flora Chilena"* by *Roberto Muñoz Pizarro*, and later *Muñoz's* daughter *Mélica* helped him a great deal in his work of identifying medicinal plants.

Maitén – **MAGTHUN** (redrawn from *Muñoz, 1959)*

Chapter 7
Medicinal Plants
1972

"Agüita de Toronjil" (Lemon balm infusion, a medicinal plant.) –
Title of song from Chilean folklore

It didn't take Robert more than two or three visits with indigenous people to begin a rather substantial list of plants that had medicinal value for use as home remedies. As the catalog grew, Robert tried to list the cures produced into categories of the specific afflictions remedied. This list included: abortion symptoms, allergies, asthma, backache, blood pressure, bronchitis, bruises, burns, calluses, cancers, colds, conjunctivitis, constipation, cough, deafness, diabetes, diarrhea, drunkenness, earache, facial paralysis, fever, flatulence, flu, fungus, gut ache, hair disorders, headache, heart palpitations (and other heart disorders), hemorrhages, hemorrhoids, indigestion, inflammation, injuries or wounds, insomnia, insect bites, intestinal gas, intestinal worms, kidney and gall stones, kidney problems (general), libido loss, mange or scabies, menstrual pain, miscarriage (prevention of), muscle spasms, nerve pain (and sciatic pain), nose bleed, rheumatism, skin disorders (irritation and rash), liver pain, sore throat, stomach ulcers, stomach ache, and warts.

It was apparent that these remedies did not necessarily cure or eliminate a specific disorder but rather alleviated the pain and suffering the ailment caused. In other words, they improved the quality of life. Some plants had curative properties against a single malady, others acted against several or even many maladies. As Robert continued his survey, he was aware that many exotic plants grown in Chile also had curative properties. Initially he focused only on native plants, as he wanted to save those remedies for posterity. This fast-growing list of medicinal plants and some major remedies are listed in the appendix.

48

The interesting feature about the plants in this list is that each had a centuries-long history of efficacy against some particular ailment(s). There didn't seem to be any obvious grouping of ailments and plant groups. As he conducted later surveys he added to this list. His aim was to only investigate native Chilean herbs as a great deal of research had already been done in other parts of the world on other herbs. So, his work was cut out for him in Chile.

His partners at Pharmtec did not initially plan to extract the active chemicals effective against these ailments. However, the initiation of their company coincided with an actively growing interest, not only in the United States in the use of effective medicinal plant and herbal remedies, but in the world in general.

So, to verify the historical efficacy of each plant, Robert collected plant samples and pressed them in a plant press to create museum-quality specimens that could be used for reference purposes in future scientific work. As he collected these plants, he made maps of their locations and followed their cycle during the growing season. Then, in late summer or fall he collected fruits, dried them and then extracted the seeds. These he would either package and send to the laboratory in Montana or take them with him in his baggage when he returned home for the northern summer.

The business in Montana was now doing quite well. Sales in Europe and the United States had increased and all of the former part-time employees were now working full-time. Several were taking special courses to increase their abilities to cope with a growing business. At Pharmtec the seeds were checked for possible pathogens and then germinated. Employees measured germination rates, cultured for possible pathogens, and recorded growth data as the young plants adjusted to the environment of the new greenhouse.

As the plants grown in the greenhouse increased in quantity, tissues were dried or extracted for crude extracts to be used as remedies. They were sold in attractive packaging showing the remedy of interest on the packing with a color picture of the plant as it appeared in Chile in its natural setting.

These extracts were sold as organic herbal remedies only and not modified. Thus, they were not subject to FDA inspections or rules. The employees at Pharmtec, though, ran a top-notch operation and seldom did a customer complain that the product they purchased had not had the desired effect on their ailment.

In early October, 1972 Robert had begun working his way eastward up the *Lonquimay* Valley, starting at *Temuco*, and then moving on to *Victoria*. As he progressed up the valley, he began to hear about a *Pehuenche* **machi** who lived further up the valley and who knew a lot about the local plant remedies. She and her husband were rather unusual as her father was a French man who came to the valley in the early 1920s and married a local girl who was viewed as a princess within the local *Pehuenche* tribe.

The family was better off financially than most in the valley and they had never moved away. There were stories about the grandfather who had come from France, broken by the First World War, and how he had come to marry into the family. There were now a son and daughter who helped their parents as well. The family spent much of their time searching out and recording local Chilean folklore music, and the wife was especially knowledgeable about medicinal plant remedies.

Several individuals told him to be sure to stop and see these people, but also to be careful of the daughter as she was very protective of her parents and was kind of mean to strangers and especially to people she didn't like.

The sign at the entrance of the road leading to the
González's home.

Chapter 8
Lonquimay Valley
October, 1972

"Soy una chispa de fuego." (I am a spark of fire.) – Song verse from Chilean folklore.

So, it was with some trepidation that Robert stopped at the driveway to the *González's* house on that bright, early spring day in October. He read the sign on the post which read, "**Lawentu chefe**," and on the second line, *Claudia G.* He knew that **Lawentu** referred to someone who dispensed medicinal plant remedies. Also, the sign showed a symbol of the Araucanian flag. He went down the driveway, crossed a small stream, and then followed the road that wound around behind a rather large house that resembled a Swiss chalet. It appeared that the main entrance was in the rear of the house. He stepped out of his vehicle and was met by a little barking dog that didn't bite but had a menacing appearance. The rear door opened and a middle-aged man came out on the porch and cheerfully said, *"Buenos días"* (Good day).

Robert introduced himself and said he was collecting medicinal plants and would he know anyone in the area who knew a lot about these plants. The man said his name was *Juan*. His wife, *Claudia*, he said, was a **machi** in the local *Pehuenche* tribe and was very knowledgeable about medicinal plants. He called back through the open door and called, *"Claudia, hay un joven aquí que quiere aprender algo de las plantas medicinales. Creo que es el que hemos estado esperando."* (*Claudia*, there is a young man here who wants to learn about medicinal plants. I think he is the one we have been expecting.)

A middle-aged woman came out of the house wiping her hands with a towel. She did not appear quite as Robert expected. While most of the *Araucanians* that Robert had previously met in his travels tended to be rather short and stocky in build, and although

Pehuenches tended to be somewhat taller, this woman was quite tall, thin, and with long, straight black hair. She was wearing modern clothing, which included a medium-length black skirt, a white blouse, a flashy necklace of silver and *lapis lazuli* gemstones, and large, matching earrings.

She extended her hand and smiled as she said in perfect English, "Hi, I'm *Claudia. Juan* says you are interested in medicinal plants. Come in, we were expecting you. We have been hearing stories about this crazy *gringo* combing southern Chile for medicinal plants. We were just going to have *hierba mate* for *once*. Although we usually drink tea, at least once a day we also drink *mate* because it's good for digestion. Today we might even have a little *guarisnaque* to celebrate your arrival here." Robert wondered to himself, "What is *guarisnaque?*" (Later that day he would learn that it was a very powerful rum beverage.) And, did *Claudia* say that she and *Juan* were expecting him? How could that be? They must have a pretty good grapevine communications system.

During the next very pleasant hour, which extended to several hours, *Juan* and *Claudia* told Robert about their recent tour in Europe playing Chilean folk music. They were going to tour less now that their daughter, *Rosa*, was studying at the University of Chile in *Santiago*. Their son *Miguel* was now living in *Santiago* and working for *CORFO*, a government department responsible for developing economic programs.

Robert explained his work in more detail, what he was doing in his survey, and what his company hoped to do with the information he collected. During his explanations, Robert thought that *Claudia* seemed to be studying him, but he didn't want to embarrass her, so every time he felt her gaze on him he would glance away and talk about some other detail of his work, addressing his attention to *Juan*.

In later years, Robert would remember that afternoon with great affection. First of all, he was impressed that he seemed to be a special guest. *Claudia* served them with her best china and a white muslin tablecloth (or *mantelito*) that she said had been in the family since the 1700s. Each place setting had a monogrammed muslin napkin, not a paper one.

Robert also noticed that all the fruits and vegetables served were cut into pieces and served on the finest china. Nothing was served unpeeled or whole. He had first noticed this when he began moving through the south of Chile searching for medicinal plants. Even the poorest country folks had treated him like an honored guest.

As Robert sat there, he reflected on his journey so far in Chile and realized that each time he stopped and had a conversation with someone in the Chilean countryside about medicinal plant remedies, he would invariably be invited to someone's house for *once*, and he was always served as a special guest, deserving of the finest china, silverware, and linen napkin. Never before in his life had he been treated with such hospitality. He recalled some houses he had entered where the floor was hard-packed dirt and its occupants obviously poor, but the houses were always immaculately clean and the floor always recently swept. And he was always welcomed!

He wanted to collect plants in this area and asked them if he could set up his tent down by the *Naranjo* River, a hundred yards or so away from their house. He would use it as a base from which to operate as he made his plant collections, but not so close that his presence would be a bother to them. When he collected as much information and plants as he felt was sufficient for that area he would move on further up the valley and continue collections there.

Claudia and *Juan* seemed to be happy to have him camp on their land. They seemed to trust him from the start and he hoped that he would not give them cause to lose that trust. During the next few weeks, Robert was delighted with his work with *Claudia* and learned a great deal about medicinal plants and the remedies associated with them. *Claudia* explained some of her work as a **machi**.

She said that **machis** had certain unexplained powers but they were difficult to understand and use. One power that she had come to

54

recognize was a certain ability to see into the future, but it was frustrating because there were never enough details and, so, she almost never recounted her premonitions to any one because neither she nor they would understand what the premonitions meant.

During the last week that Robert was there, camped with his little tent alongside the river, he heard a bus drive up and stop at the turnoff road to the *González's* driveway. The little dog ran toward the bus as a young lady stepped out, carrying a small travel bag. *"Chao Don Eduardo"* she said to the driver, and he replied, *"Chao, Señorita, saludos a sus padres."* She walked up the road to the house, not too far from where he was preparing plants that he had collected that day. He had to stop and watch, and thought to himself, "Boy, is she good looking!"

Her aquiline facial features suggested Arabian or Moorish blood somewhere in her ancestry. She was dressed like a university student. It must be *Rosa!* *Claudia* had said that she was a student at the University of Chile in *Santiago.* It was very unusual for a country girl from such a remote location in Chile to be accepted as a student at such a prestigious university, but *Juan* and *Claudia* had used their influence as nationally known folk singers to help her gain admission.

Robert returned to his work, removing pressed plants from his presses, labeling them, and packing them between pieces of cardboard for eventual shipment to the States. He was absorbed in his work and was startled when he heard a young girl's voice say in a rather accusatory tone in English, "So, you are the *gringuito* who is stealing my mother's medicinal plant remedies? You should be ashamed of yourself. All you *gringos* seem to want to do is come to Chile and steal our resources! First it was bird guano, then copper, gold and silver, and now you come."

A startled Robert looked up and was overwhelmed by her appearance and closeness. He had never seen such beautiful brown eyes! Her eyes had such depth that he thought he could look right into them and not see the bottom. All he could do in reaction was to blurt out, "God, you are beautiful!" But, she quickly recovered her advantage and replied, "I know, but you are not talking to God, you are talking to me." Then they both laughed and she extended her hand.

"My name is *Rosa*," she said, "and I guess you have heard of me. *Soy muy guapa! Ten cuidado gringuito!*" (I am very tough! Be careful little gringo!). "But, I guess I will have to accept you for awhile as my mother seems to be infatuated with you. She wanted me to tell you to come up to the house and that you are invited for *once*."

Robert had enjoyed *once* at the *González's* house many times in the past several weeks but this one was even more enjoyable. *Rosa* explained her studies at the university. She was a freshman, majoring in economics, and her brother *Miguel* had been studying political science but had married, had two children, and was now working with *CORFO* in *Santiago*.

CORFO, or *Corporación de Fomento*, was a government agency responsible for developing economic programs or projects to assist the growth of the Chilean economy. *Miguel* loved his job and was active with some of his political friends, demonstrating for social justice and welfare. He was a great supporter of the new president, *Salvador Allende*. *Miguel* was a good friend of a university professor and famous folk singer named *Víctor Jara* who was also very active in campaigning for social justice.

What a wonderful family the *González's* seemed to be! Before he left to return to his tent, they brought out their guitars, a harp, and sang a series of folklore songs. The singing went on for several hours, along with much drinking of wine.

When Robert got up to leave, he stumbled and almost fell to the floor. He had drunk more than he should have and was a little ashamed. *Rosa* offered to help him down to his tent and as he began to lie down on his sleeping bag he accidently, or perhaps not so accidently, touched her hip with his hand.

She gently removed it and said, *"Gringuito, no señor, tu eres muy simpático, pero yo soy intocable, especialmente por un gringo que quiere robarle a nuestra gente sus riquezas."* (No, Mr. *Gringo*, you are a nice guy, but I am untouchable, especially by a *gringo* who wants to rob our people of our plant health remedies!)

Then she laughed, pinched his now red cheek, and returned to the house. Robert slept like a log that night, thinking about not only about the parasitic *misodendrum* plants but also a little bit about *Rosa*. Now, Robert was a very shy young man and would have never made advances to a young lady. But, during the rest of his life, and especially during the next few years, he would often and fondly recall that day and realize with much satisfaction that that was the day he fell in love with *Rosa González*.

Since the first time that Robert had seen *misodendrum* plants he had been fascinated by them. This was a group of parasitic flowering plants that existed by parasitizing branches of living *Nothofagus* trees. Their natural range is from *Santiago* southward to *Tierra del Fuego* but only at a certain altitude in the Andean *Cordillera*. They are found nowhere else in the world. These interesting parasites had evolved in their own small corner of the world in southern Chile and a part of southern Argentina.

When Robert asked *Claudia* about them she seemed a little troubled by his question and initially put him off without a detailed explanation. She said that the plants had some remedial properties that she did not understand, but that her great grandmother had referred to them as very powerful for certain diseases, but she was reluctant to say much except that they could be very dangerous if not used carefully.

At any rate, Robert collected samples, pressed them, and preserved other tissue samples to send back to the States. The plants of *misodendrum* were very abundant at a certain altitudinal level on the slopes of the *Lonquimay* Volcano and rather rare at lower elevations. They were abundant at lower altitudes farther south in Chile.

The family of Misodendraceae contains only one genus, and all species are shrubby branch parasites of higher plants, mostly *Nothofagus spp.* The subgenus *Angelopogon* contains four species and the subgenus *Misodendrum* contains seven species. Available evidence suggests that

Misodendrum may represent the oldest extant genus that evolved the mistletoe habit. Most of the *misodendrum* species have scale-like leaves or very abbreviated linear leaves. Those with scale-like leaves have stems that are usually a golden yellow in color and those with linear leaves are either golden or greenish in color.

Misodendrum flowers are not very visible until after they are fertilized. Then each developing fruit produces three long, feathery appendages, perhaps four inches or more in length. These appendages are very flexible and, when the seed is released, their increased friction with the air helps the seed to be carried long distances by the wind. Then they help the seed become attached to a susceptible branch by the wind by wrapping the filament around the branch. In function, they behave much as a spider's thread spun into the wind, eventually able to carry the weight of the spider some distance simply because of friction with the moving air.

Before seed dispersal, clusters of these long, feathery growths are highly visible from far away. This led early plant collectors to classify *misodendrum* plants as "the feathery mistletoes", *"Barba del Roble"* (Oak's beard) or *"Cabello de Angel"* (Angel's hair) and witches' brooms.

At the beginning of the Chilean winter in April of 1972, Robert returned for a brief visit to the States. He generally didn't work in the field in winter in the southern hemisphere, especially in southern Chile, because although the winters weren't all that cold, it rained and snowed a lot and camping in a tent could be very uncomfortable. So, he returned to the States to visit his parents and touch base with scientists at Pharmtec to see how the work was going.

When Robert was a graduate student, he did his thesis research on a species of dwarf mistletoe that was parasitic on the Douglas-fir tree. Dwarf mistletoes are distant relatives of the *misodendrums*. One finding of his research was that the dwarf mistletoe converted carbon dioxide in air, and the carbon in sugars derived from the host, to produce large volumes of lipids. He didn't know the significance of this but thought that the plant used fixation of carbon into the relatively inert lipid materials to help maintain a strong nutrient gradient from the host into the parasite. The inert lipid could then be quickly mobilized by the mistletoe plant, when needed, and converted into energy for flowering and fruiting.

Scientists at Pharmtec made some preliminary extractions of the *misodendrum* samples he had brought with him and found them to be rich in a certain kind of lipid known as essential oil. This was an interesting finding as many medicinal plants have essential oils as their effective medicinal component. They were going to need more samples and "would Robert please collect a lot more from where he got these, and also from different host species."

And, "oh by the way, his draft number was very high and it was certain that he would have to enter the military as soon he returned." His draft board told him that he would probably get a better deal if he enlisted as long as he returned by February.

Robert returned to the valley that summer in early September to the overture of much unrest in *Santiago*. Wealthier citizens were upset with the rise in food prices and there were public demonstrations almost every day against the *Allende* regime. Rumors were increasing that the military might force out *Allende* in some kind of coup.

Juan and *Claudia* were happy to see him again and *Rosa* was there as well, and not in school. The university had closed because of the almost daily student demonstrations. Again, she was not very happy to see him. *Miguel* had told her that the Nixon presidency was secretly sending money to Chile to help undermine *Allende's* attempts at installing Socialism in Chile. Nixon was actually sending money covertly to Chile to fund much of the social unrest and public demonstrations. Could this be true? Robert doubted it but didn't want to offend her so he said nothing. Many years later he would learn that this was, indeed, true.

Robert was getting ready to pack up his tent in preparation for his trip back to the States the next day. As he was concluding his packing he heard a sharp scream. He emerged from the tent and looked around. The screams were coming from the *Naranjo* River. This was spring and snowmelt had turned the river into a raging torrent, heading toward a much bigger river, the *Biobío*.

Rosa was running along the bank on the south side of the river and screaming "*¡Mamá, Mamá!*" Robert jumped up without putting on his boots and ran over near to where she was screaming and hollered, "What's wrong?" She screamed, "*Mamá* was chasing some sheep near the river bank and the bank collapsed and she fell in. The current is fast and she can't swim well!"

Their little dog, *Quinto*, had already jumped in and was swimming toward *Claudia*. Robert tore off his shirt and ran along the bank as the current bore *Claudia* along. He saw a mass of brush a little farther along and knew he had to save her before she became entangled in the brush.

He jumped in headfirst and swam toward her. He didn't quite make it before *Claudia* was swept into the tree's branches. Her feet apparently became entangled in the submerged branches and the current pulled her under as the rushing water swept over her.

Robert knew that he would probably not be able to free her feet from the branches but he had to get her head above water or she would soon drown. As he came alongside the spot where she had disappeared he groped under the water and grabbed her hair. He tried to pull her free and swim away, but all he could do was to hold her head above water, and was barely able to hang onto both her and a tree branch.

He had never worked harder in his life as he held *Claudia's* face above the water with one hand and with his other hand held onto branches to keep from being swept away. The swift current continuously splashed waves over his head and he was not able to see what *Rosa* was doing. And he was quickly becoming hypothermic! *Claudia* was struggling to help him keep her head above the water. He suspected that she was also becoming hypothermic but she was still pretty actively trying to stay alive.

60

After what seemed like an eternity, and as he began to lose consciousness, he sensed several hands helping him to hold onto *Claudia*. Out of the corner of his eye he saw a man backing a yoke of oxen down the bank and toward the tree. Soon, other pairs of hands were hooking a logging chain to the tree. Years later, Robert recalled very few further details of that day, but for some unknown reason, he never forgot the names of the two oxen as their master urged them to pull, *"¡Hia, Pajarito, hia Flor!"* (Get going Little Bird, get going Flower!)

As the oxen walked away, they easily pulled the tree out of the water and both *Claudia* and Robert collapsed onto the bank. *Claudia* was immediately wrapped in a blanket and *Rosa* broke down in tears as she hugged her mother. *Rosa* cradled her mother in her arms and sobbed, *"Mamá*, are you okay?" *Claudia* choked a little but soon started breathing more easily and she and *Claudia* began to cry, now out of joy and not out of fear. She choked again and said, "I thought I was going to drown. Robert saved me." And then she looked at *Rosa* as she continued, "What a gentleman he is. Thank you, Robert." But Robert didn't feel too good. He was chilled to the bone, nauseous, and had a terrific headache.

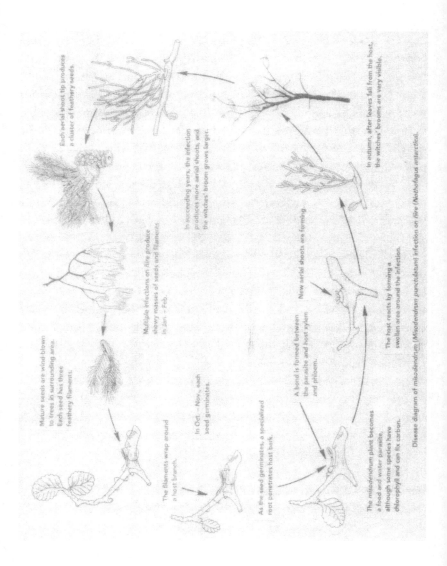

Mature seeds are wind-blown to trees in surrounding area. Each seed has three feathery filaments.

The filaments wrap around a host branch.

In Oct. – Nov., each seed germinates.

As the seed germinates, a specialized root penetrates host bark.

Each aerial shoot tip produces a cluster of feathery seeds.

Multiple infections on *fire* produce showy masses of seeds and filaments in Jan. – Feb.

In succeeding years, the infection produces more aerial shoots, and the witches' broom grows larger.

In autumn, after leaves fall from the host, the witches' brooms are very visible.

New aerial shoots are forming.

A bond is formed between the parasite and host xylem and phloem.

The host reacts by forming a swollen area around the infection.

The *misodendrum* plant becomes a food and water parasite, although some species have chlorophyll and can fix carbon.

Disease diagram of misodendrum (*Misodendrum punctulatum*) infection on *fire* (*Nothofagus antarctica*).

62

Chapter 9
Rosa

"Love of my life, *eres tú, eres tú*." (It is you, it is you.) – Verse
from "Touch the Wind", the English version of the popular Latin
American song *"Eres tú, eres tú."*

Later that day, Robert developed a fever and felt quite ill. He obviously could not stay alone in his tent. He had probably contracted flu or pneumonia when his body was weakened by hypothermia in the water. The *González's* insisted that he stay with them and he was ushered into a spare bedroom. During the night he became delirious.

When he awoke the next morning the fever had gone and he was aware that *Claudia* and *Rosa* were sitting on either side of the bed. *Claudia* said she had given him an infusion of **Palqui** and that was what had broken the fever. Robert was interested in the plant since he had not yet collected it. He rapidly recovered from his illness that day and he had the name of another medicinal plant to add to his list. And this was one that was actually used on him, so he could speak from experience.

There was a lot of laughter that night at supper. Robert had never felt so satisfied with his life. He was an honored guest for that meal, and a lot of neighbors attended as well, each bringing a little something to eat or drink. He was supposed to leave the next morning, but *Claudia* suggested that he stay a day or two longer and that he and *Rosa* should visit the sacred Araucaria pine grove on their land up behind the mountain in back of the house. There were some other *misodendrum* species there that he might like to collect. There were very interesting infections on *canelo*, a small tree species that was now a very rarely encountered host of *misodendrum*.

So, early the next morning, *Claudia* helped Robert saddle his horse. They stopped by the house and picked up the lunch that *Claudia* had prepared. They rode their horses up a trail on the mountain in back of the house and crossed to a valley beyond another mountain. As they trotted along the mountain trail, the absence of the little dog tugged at their hearts, he had become entangled in the brush and had drowned while Robert was trying to rescue *Claudia*.

As they rode up the trail to the top of the first mountain, Robert was overjoyed to see the expanse of the virgin, old-growth Araucaria pine forest and to be riding among many large trees, most of them hundreds of years old, and others thousands of years old. What treasures! But, several mountains to the south, this forest was under attack by a large consortium from *Santiago* that was trying to confiscate the land to harvest the trees. Dropping into the second valley, he found *misodendrum* plants on some of the understory shrubs that were not the usual hosts such as the *Nothofagus* trees that he had collected from before. *Rosa* said that this area was a relic from a past glaciation and there were many plant species here that today only occurred much farther to the south. This was the area that *Claudia* had mentioned.

Rosa took Robert to the small grove of *canelo* trees that were considered sacred by the Araucanian Indians. Robert was thrilled to find several *canelo* trees infected with *misodendrum*. This was specifically *Misodendrum brachystachyum*, which had linear, leatherlike green leaves. He had never seen any *misodendrum* on *canelo* before. He collected a few leaves and placed them in his plant press, being careful to not disturb the *misodendrum* stem itself and the infection site. He realized that this find was a great treasure and began to consider what he might do to propagate both host and parasite and increase their geographic ranges.

Claudia had prepared a delicious basket lunch and *Rosa* was on her best behavior. She was thrilled to see Robert's reaction to the *misodendrum* parasitizing *canelo*. Robert thought that *Rosa* was actually being quite nice to him and for once she seemed to enjoy being with him. What happened next is something that Robert would recall many times during the rest of his life. Aspects of this memory would keep him alive during the next year when he was in Vietnam.

He probably had a little too much to drink and before he realized it, his eyes began to droop and he could not stop himself from falling asleep. As he fell asleep, he thought he saw *Rosa* watching him. Robert suddenly awoke, but could not move. He could open his eyes but could barely move his legs or arms. He said, "*Rosa*, what the hell is going on? Did you drug me? What is happening to me?" *Rosa* laughed and said, "So, the *gringuito* is awake, huh?"

She came over to where he was lying, very deliberately kneeled down, and taking his face between her hands, kissed him full on the lips. Now, Robert was not exactly a ladies man but he had kissed a few girls when he was in college although he had never seriously dated anyone. This was a kiss like none he had ever experienced before! She had kissed him full on the lips and when their lips met it seemed as though she drew something from his being. She caressed his face and kissed him again.

Then she unbuckled his belt and began sliding his pants down his legs. As she did so she smiled at him. She slid off his socks and underwear. As she removed his underwear he saw what he had realized as he awakened, that he had the largest, hardest erection that he had ever had in his life. What had she given him? Was it in the wine? And he couldn't move or do anything, except watch her. Why was she doing this? Was she crazy? She carefully folded his pants and shorts and laid them on the blanket next to their lunch basket.

She then dropped down to her hands and knees crawled toward him, all the while looking into his eyes. He would never forget those flashing brown eyes, those eyes that had a depth you could see into. She said, "*Roberto*, I love my parents more than anything in this world, I especially love my mother as only a daughter can love her mother. I almost lost her yesterday and you gave her back to me. You are a fine young man but you are very shy. Since I will probably never

65

see you again, I want to share with you something that is precious to me."

She then slowly slipped off her riding britches and carefully folded them and placed them on the blanket next to his folded clothes. She removed her panties and lifted her shirt, holding it up around her hips. As she lifted her legs to straddle him he saw that she was as excited as he was. He thought, "What in the hell is going on here?"

She gently positioned herself over him. He detected a faint musky scent as she lowered herself onto his penis, letting him slide in all the way, and then moving gently up and down. He had an orgasm almost immediately, certainly faster than he wanted and, as he passed out again, he heard her say, "*Roberto*, I am giving you a part of me, and this is my gift to you for giving me back my mother. I have behaved rather badly to you, and this is the least I can do to make amends. Thank you, *Roberto*, for giving me back my mother. She is the most precious thing I have in my life."

The rest of the afternoon passed too quickly for the both of them. Robert soon regained his ability to move and they made love again twice more until finally Robert was so tired that he could hardly move. On several occasions he wanted to tell *Rosa* that he loved her, but then he remembered all that had happened that day and before and he forced it out of his mind.

Later, in Vietnam, he would regret that decision. Besides, at that time he wasn't yet sure that he really loved her. Maybe he would say something later. *Rosa* seemed to be not at all tired and when Robert mentioned the fact, she laughed and said, "Someday I will be a **machi,** and they have many unusual talents." "Speaking of unusual talents, what was that drug that you gave me? I have never heard of such a thing and it was so powerful," he asked.

She replied, "Dear *Roberto*, there are many things that you do not yet know about medicinal plants. **Palwe** is a rarely known and rarely used herb that greatly increases sexual desire. You know that it is not used much in Chile because it is not necessary. We Chileans don't need it." Robert thought about that for a while and made a mental note to find out more about **Palwe**. *Rosa* said no more about it but winked at him as he thought about what she had said just now.

They talked a great deal about almost everything that afternoon. Robert had already told her about the draft and that if he enlisted he might get a less dangerous assignment. For the rest of his life Robert would regret that decision. *Rosa* suggested that he stay in Chile and not enter the military service. But he said he had to go, and that he would be back as soon as he could after his year of service. At any rate, she was going to return to the university and hoped that the demonstrations supporting *Allende* had stopped so that classes could begin again. She said that her mother was afraid of what was going to happen in Chile, for *Juan*, and for her, and for *Miguel*.

Laurel de Campo – TRIWEE (redrawn from Muñoz, 1959)

Chapter 10
Folk Singing
1940's to 1960's

"Levántate Huenchullán" (Rise *Huenchullán,* one of the *Mapuche* heroes from the time of the Spanish conquest.) – Verse from the protest song *"Arauco tiene una pena"* composed by *Violeta Parra*

During the night flight back to the States, Robert had a series of persistent dreams, about *Rosa* of course, but the music that *Juan* and *Claudia* had introduced him to kept pounding in his head. It was such a rich experience that he could not stop from remembering song titles and verses, in a cacophony of musical vibrations. It was obvious that both *Claudia* and *Juan* had an instinctive love of music, especially that of their native Chile. Chileans are by nature a happy people. Although many are rather poor financially, they typically are wonderfully circumspect of their socio-financial condition and seek humor wherever they can find it, regardless of their social or economic positions, and much of that humor comes out in the form of songs.

During Robert's many visits to their home, the *González's* had shared their love of folklore music with him, explaining the history and purpose of every song. They knew all the current folk singers and sometimes one or more of these would pass by their house and much singing would result. There were many singing groups during the 1960s and 70s. The more popular ones included: *El Conjunto Cuncumén, El Conjunto Millaray, Las Cuatro Brujas, Los Cuatro Cuartos, Los de Ramón, Los Huasos Quincheros, Los Jaivas,* and *Las Conejitas* (for children's songs). And there were many more.

Juan and *Claudia* explained to Robert that there are basically three groupings of Chilean folklore music: (1) music from *Santiago,* the capital, and other cities, that has a distinctive quality and might include both wealthy and poor people; (2) music from the countryside, which

68

mainly includes people who were born and lived in the country, most of whom are poor or, at the least, live lives filled with hardship; and (3) music of the native aborigines, the Araucanian Indians, who had lived on the land which is now Chile at least 14,000 years before the arrival of Europeans. To a smaller extent, this group also includes music of Rapa-Nui, Easter Island, which was annexed by Chile in the mid-1800s.

Chilean folklore music was generally music of the common people, mostly written by and for people of the *campo*, or countryside. They celebrated the social life of families, such as in *"Mi abuela bailó sirilla"*, or a wedding, *"El casorio"*. They describe the happy time of courtship such as in *"Poema 20 de Pablo Neruda"*, *"Ojitos de agua dulce"*, *"Ende que te vi"*, or *"Niña de cara morena"*.

Romance plays a large part in Chilean folklore. A young man's first love is described in *"Ende que te vi"*. *"Qué bonita va"* describes the beauty of a young girl. With you I will go, in *"Contigo me voy"*.

More sadness was expressed in songs such as a reflection on the unmarried pregnant daughter in *"Huija"*, or just to generally suffer in *"Sufrir"*, the lonely man in *"El solitario"*, sadness of the soul in *"Qué pena siente el alma"*. Loneliness in general is covered in *"Camino de soledad"* and love and sorrow in *"Una pena y un cariño"*.

"El huaso ladino" is about an honest cowboy. *"Mocosita"* is about a young girl who abandons a man who loves her. *"Pa' mar adentro"* is about the life of fishermen. A martyr is lamented in *"El martirio"*. A couple of good buddies are celebrated in *"Los compadres paleteados"*. Revenge is described in *"El guatón Loyola"* in which a bully is trapped under a table in a bar and punched by all of his so-called friends in punishment for being such a bully.

Chilean folklore also recognizes the importance that material things like tools play in the lives of country folk. Examples are: a wool cap in *"El gorro de lana"*, a red rose in *"Rosa colorada"*, a happy smoking pipe in *"Cachimbo alegre"*, large pots in *"Cantarito de Peñaflor"*, a white tablecloth in *"Mantelito blanco"*, a three colored poncho in *"Manta de tres colores"*, silver spurs in *"Espuelas de plata"*, a foot path in *"Senderito"*, or a small adobe house in *"Ranchito de totora"*. *"Aradito de palo"* recognizes the importance of this essential tool, a wooden plow, in the life of a farmer. A tool from which to drink *mate* can be either a simple gourd or a much fancier affair. In *"Matecito de plata"*, an elaborate silver-adorned gourd that the family used long ago is remembered, and lamented with great nostalgia, by the person who wrote the words many years ago.

Chileans are extremely nationalistic and remember their history with great affection, such as songs of the War of the Pacific in 1879-1883 in *"Batallones olvidados"*, old battle flags in *Los viejos estandartes"*, or a female Chilean spy living in Peru in *"Romance de Leonora Latorre"*. The cavalry, again probably reminiscent of the War of the Pacific, is celebrated in *"Canción de la caballería"*.

There are happy times too, though, such as in *"Santiago está de fiesta"*, or the *cueca,* a popular country dance, in *"Apología de la cueca"*, or if you are going to Chile, in *"Si vas para Chile"*.

Some songs are simply silly, such as *"La rana"*, in which the adventures of a frog are elaborated upon. *"El Diablo se fue a bañar"* describes the adventures of the devil who finally meets his match in the singer's mother-in-law.

A young man remembers, with fondness, the priest in the little village where he grew up, in *"Cura de mi pueblo"*. Another man remembers the fondness he had felt when working with wood, in *"Tallando"*. A young man recalls the thrill he felt every time a young girl showed her petticoat, in *"La enagüita"*. Another young woman admits that she is in love with the sacristan, the young man who assists the priest, in *"El sacristán"*.

Chilean folklore can also be quite sad and nostalgic, such as in *"Mi viejo"* or *"Porque tengo pena"* or love and hate, in *"Una pena y un cariño"* or sadness of the soul, in *"Qué pena siente el alma"*.

A particularly sad song is *"El corralero,"* in which a worker at a ranch is told by his foreman to take the old horse out to the field and cut its throat because it is old and has outlived its usefulness. The singer laments his task and recalls that the horse worked so hard during its life and actually had been the most intelligent of all the horses on the ranch. As he goes to the shed to get the machete, the horse follows him and nuzzles him as he sharpens the knife. The man then realizes that he cannot kill the horse. Instead, he decides that he will take care of it himself, until the horse dies of old age.

Juan and *Claudia* began to sing to the public in 1963 at a music festival in *Viña del Mar*. They called themselves "*Los de Juan*", perhaps not very original, but two other family groups, *Los de Ramón* and the *Conjunto Cuncumén*, had become very popular singing Chilean folklore music, and so they thought, why not. They were a family group too. When they were only small children, *Miguel* and *Rosa* danced the *cueca* while their parents played various country songs. Later the children would play instruments with their parents as a family group.

Although the family started their music career playing all popular Chilean songs, they began to focus first on old songs of the Araucarian Indians, and then on the songs expressing the social unrest that had begun to surge across the working class in Chile. In an important aspect the theme of both types of music was identical, a cry from an oppressed and downtrodden group of citizens. As they joined voices and hearts with other popular contemporary musicians such as *Violeta Parra* and *Víctor Jara*, their outcry began to be heard.

In 1969, they made an extensive tour of Chile, Argentina, and Peru. In 1970, they toured Brazil, and later in that year they toured in Spain, France, and The Netherlands. In 1972, they returned to Paris where they gave a recital at the Olympia Theater and continued on a 60-day tour of Belgium, Germany, Spain, France, and the Soviet Union. In early 1973, they returned to Chile and to their home in *Lonquimay* to recuperate and to begin to make record albums of the songs they had collected.

There was always an abundance of poor people in Chile. They survived by living in an almost medieval top-down economy, doing menial work for relatively poor salaries or wages. World War Two resulted in a lot of money going into the world economy and some of this reached to the Chilean economy. But by the early 1960s this stimulus was losing steam. The population had grown and the feeling was that wealthy people were doing well but the majority was not doing so well.

The new president, *Eduardo Frei Montalva*, embraced the Alliance for Progress championed by the U. S. President John F. Kennedy. But *Frei* made some big mistakes by confiscating some productive farmlands from hard-working owners and then parceling them out to the poor, many of whom either did not know how to farm or were simply lazy. These actions began to alienate the wealthy. Perhaps this was also partially a result of widespread use of the radio and television as more people could see and hear how well other people were doing. A growing demand arose in Chile declaring that the poor people deserved a life with more quality in it, and their voices clamored louder than those of the wealthy. A call for socialism thus arose in Chile. Vocal critics called it Communism and this triggered even more intolerance from the upper classes. Folk singers were quick to come to the aid of the poor and disenfranchised.

Although several singers began to retrieve and collect the old country songs, which became known as folklore, only one had a true passion for the poor and the misery of the lives in which they were entrapped. That person was *Violeta Parra*.

Born in 1917 as *Violeta del Carmen Parra Sandoval*, she eventually followed the legend of her father, an important folklorist in the region of *Ñuble*. *Violeta* had eight brothers and two half-brothers. When she was still young her father lost his job. Her mother had to maintain the family by doing anything she could, such as washing and mending clothes, and selling and buying what she could to help her family survive. The children also did what they could and began singing for their friends and charging admission. They sang in trains, restaurants and anyplace where people were gathered, going as far as Chillán and Parral.

72

At age twelve *Violeta* composed her first songs and accompanied them on the guitar. At age 20 she went to *Santiago* and continued her hard life there, singing in small bars, circuses, theaters, on the radio, and wherever she could find an audience. Although it was a difficult life, she began to take an interest in Chilean country music.

Her big chance came in 1953 when she sang a recital in the house of *Pablo Neruda*. *Radio Chilena* was impressed with her performance and commissioned her to collect Chilean folklore music. She spent the next year traveling the length of Chile seeking out local folklore music and recording it for posterity. In 1954, she was awarded the *Caupolicán* Prize as folklorist of the year.

As a consequence, she was invited to Poland and the Soviet Union and she lived for two years in Paris. When she returned, she lived in *Concepción* and *Santiago*, singing and recording her songs. She also began to paint and weave, and traveled again to Europe and other countries to exhibit her songs and artwork.

Several folk singers had begun to address the challenge of poverty in Chile. *Violeta Parra* was a person coping with personal problems, having had two marriages and a lost love, but also bursting with compassion for the common people, especially the poor.

The earlier songs of *Violeta Parra* represent perhaps the most melancholy of all Chilean music, even those sung by native Chileans, lamenting the loss of the past and their land. Two songs which represent *Violata Parra's* sadness are "What have I gained by loving you?" (*"Qué he sacado con quererte"*), representing her loss of a lover who apparently did her wrong, and *"Veintiuno son los dolores"* in which she claims that she feels 21 wounds from a broken love affair.

Violeta was, by nature, a sad person, and probably suffering from bi-polar disorder. The songs she created represent her moments of brilliantness, inspired by interludes of deep despair. On February 5, 1967, during one of these desperate moments, she committed suicide at the age of 50.

Violeta had been quick to recognize the growing dissatisfaction in her beloved Chile during the 1960s. She produced a number of melancholy songs reflecting the state of the common people and their growing dissatisfaction with that condition. Perhaps the song which best describes this recognition is *"La carta"*.

Me mandaron una carta	They sent me a letter
por el correo temprano,	by the early mail,
en esa carta me dicen	in this letter I'm told
que cayó preso mi hermano,	that my brother is in jail,
y sin compasión, con grillos,	and shackled, without compassion,
por la calle lo arrastraron, si.	they dragged him down the street, yes.
La carta dice el motive	The letter says that the motive
de haber cometido Roberto	for the arrest of Roberto
haber apoyado el paro	was that he supported the strike
que ya se había resuelto.	that since had been resolved,
Si acaso esto es un motivo	In case that this is the motive
presa voy también, sargento, si.	then I will also go to jail, sergeant, yes.
Yo que me encuentro tan lejos	I am so far away
esperando una noticia,	waiting for news,
me viene a decir la carta	this letter arrives and tells me
que en mi patria no hay justicia,	that in my country there is no justice,
los hambrientos piden pan,	the hungry ask for bread,
plomo les da la milicia, si.	the military responds with lead, yes.
De esta manera pomposa	In this pompous manner
quieren conservar su asiento	they want to keep their position
los de abanico y de frac,	those who use fans and wear fancy coats,
sin tener merecimiento, si.	without deserving them, yes.
Habráse visto insolencia,	Have you ever seen such insolence,
barbarie y alevosía,	barbarity and treachery,
de presentar el Trabuco	to present the blunderbuss
y matar a sangre fría	and kill in cold blood
a quien defensa no tiene	people who are powerless

con las dos manos vacias, si.	with both hands empty, yes.
La carta que he recibido	The letter I received
me pide contestación,	requests an answer,
yo pido que se propale	I ask that they divulge
por toda la población,	for all the population,
que el {León} es un sanguinario	that the {lion}[2] is blood thirsty
en toda generación, si.	in each generation, yes.
Por suerte tengo guitarra	Luckily I have a guitar
para llorar mi dolor,	to cry away my sorrow,
también tengo nueve hermanos	I also have nine brothers
fuera del que se engrilló,	besides the one who is in jail,
los nueve son comunistas	the nine are Communists
con el favor de mi Dios, si.	by God's favor, yes.

This is a terribly sad, and even bitter, song, but it is probably not the one by which we should remember *Violeta Parra*. Perhaps one should, rather, pay tribute to one of the brightest products of her tormented life, the song, *"Gracias a la vida"*, which seems to run counter to her sadness. It is a song of hope and extreme happiness as the singer expresses her gratefulness for the blessings she has enjoyed in her life.

"Gracias a la vida, que me ha dado tanto

Thanks to life, that has given me so much

Me dio dos luceros, que cuando los abro

It has given me two eyes, that when I open them

Perfecto distingo lo negro del blanco

I clearly distinguish black from white

Y en el alto cielo, su fondo estrellado

And I can see the high sky with its starry depths

---

2 Nickname of the then President Alessandri

Y en las multitudes, el hombre que yo amo

> And among many people, the one I love

Gracias a la vida, que me ha dado tanto

> Thanks to life, that has given me so much

Me ha dado el sonido y el abecedario

> It has given sound and, with it, the alphabet

Con él las palabras que pienso y declaro

> And with it the words that I think and state

Madre, amigo, hermano, y luz alumbrando

> Father, friend, brother, and light shining on

La ruta del alma del que estoy amando

> The road of the soul of the one I love

Gracias a la vida, que me ha dado tanto

> Thanks to life, that has given me so much

Me dio el corazón, que agita su marco

> Life gave me a heart that trembles within its constraints

Cuando miro el fruto del cerebro humano

> When I observe the fruits of the human brain

Cuando miro el bueno tan lejos del malo

> When I observe the good so far from the bad

Cuando miro el fondo de sus ojos claros

> When I observe the depth of your clear eyes

Gracias a la vida, que me ha dado tanto

> Thanks to life, that has given me so much

Me ha dado la risa y me ha dado el llanto

> Life has given me laughter and it has given me tears

Así yo distingo dicha de quebranto

> Thus I can distinguish happiness from sadness

Los dos materiales que forman mi canto

> The two substances that make up my song

El canto de ustedes, que es el mismo canto

> Your song, that is the same song

El canto de todos, que es mi propio canto

> The song of everyone, that is my own song

Gracias a la vida

> Thanks for life

Gracias a la vida"

> Thanks for life

After a lifetime of sadness and many sad songs, perhaps this song of joy is the one song by which we should remember *Violeta Parra*.

A large portion of Chilean folklore songs has always reflected a brutal reality of the hardships of life for the common and, especially, poor people. A whole new sense of grief and despair was reflected in Chilean folklore just a few years before the military coup in 1973. As President *Allende* struggled to socialize his political agenda, much resistance was stimulated by the wealthy. The United States encouraged public unrest in Chile by funding and encouraging demonstrations. This caused economic hardship for business owners and they, in turn, demanded that the police control this civil unrest, which they were unable to do.

Both sides committed violence. Critics began to be killed, or simply disappear. New songs reflected this violence, sometimes in subtle ways. An example is given in *"Arriba en la cordillera"* when a disappeared father's body is found up in the mountains with two bullets in his chest, a metaphorical reference to the thousands of people who began to disappear after the coup began in the following decade.

On September 11, 1973, another folk singer and champion of human rights, *Víctor Jara*, was informed as to what was happening in downtown *Santiago*. He rushed to the State Technical University where he worked as a teacher. He joined a group of students in a show of solidarity against the ongoing coup. They remained in demonstration all night. The next day the university was assaulted by military forces, many students were shot outright, and *Víctor Jara* was taken prisoner. He and many surviving students were taken to the National Soccer Stadium and detained as political dissidents.

Rumors had it that his captors taunted him, his hands were smashed, and eventually chopped off, but apparently not all of that was true. But he was taunted to play the guitar with his now-injured hands. He would not, or could not, cooperate with them and one of his captors then shot him in the head. His body was found on September 18 by his wife, one among many in a pile of cadavers. Someone counted 44 bullet holes in his body.

Víctor Jara was a genius as a writer of protest songs, and his songs subtly, and not so subtly, reflect his dissatisfaction with the worsening economic situation in Chile. It is less subtly elaborated on in a medly of songs written and sung by him, such as: *"La canción del martillo"*, *"El aparecido y el soldado"*, *"¿Quien mató a Carmencita?"*, *"Ni chicha ni limoná"* and many, many more.

A classic protest song of *Víctor Jara* was *"Movil-Oil Special"*.

Los estudiantes chilenos	The Chilean students
y latinoamericanos	and Latin American students
se tomaron de la mano	took each other by the hand
mata tire tirun dín	kill, shoot, shootie,
En este hermoso jardín	In this beautiful garden
a momios y dinosaurios	to extreme right wingers and reactionaries
los jóvenes revolucionarios	those young revolutionaries
han dicho BASTA – Por fin-.	have said ENOUGH – Finally.
Que viene el guanaco (Movil-oil Special)	There comes the water cannon truck
y detrás los pacos (Movil-oil Special)	and behind them, the police
la bomba delante (Movil-oil Special)	the tear gas in front

la paralizante (Movil-oil Special)	the paralyzing bomb
también la purgante (Movil-oil Special)	and also the laxative bomb
y la hilarante (Movil-oil Special)	and the laughing gas bomb
ay, que son cargantes (Movil-oil Special)	oh, they are so tiresome
estos vigilantes (Movil-oil Special)	these policemen
el joven secundario (Movil-oil Special)	the secondary student
y el universitario (Movil-oil Special)	and the university student
con el proletario (Movil-oil Special)	with the proletariat
quieren revolución.	they want revolution.
En la Universidad	In the University
se lucha por la reforma	they fight for the reform
para poner en la horma	to hold back
al beato y al nacional.	sanctimonious and chauvinistic people.
Somos los reformistas	We are the reformers
los revolucionarios	the revolutionaries
los anti-imperialistas	the anti-imperialists
de la Universidad.	of the University.

After hearing this song, and its message, there is little doubt as to what the military *junta* thought about *Víctor Jara*.

But, as with *Violeta Parra*, there are many other beautiful songs by which we should remember *Víctor Jara*. Said to be one of the most beautiful in Latin America is: *Te Recuerdo Amanda*.

Te recuerdo Amanda	I remember you Amanda
la calle mojada	the wet street
corriendo a la fábrica	running to the factory
donde trabajaba Manuel.	where Manuel worked.
La sonrisa ancha	The broad smile
la lluvia en el pelo	the rain in your hair
no importaba nada	with nothing else on your mind
ibas a encontrarte con él	you were going to be with him

con él, con él....	with him, with him…
Con él	With him
son cinco minutos	only five minutes
la vida es eternal	life is eternal
en cinco minutos	in five minutes
suena la sirena	the siren wails
de vuelta al trabajo	in returning to work
y tu caminando	and you walking
lo iluminas todo	you illuminate all
los cinco minutos	those five minutes
te hacen florecer.	make you bloom like a flower.
Te recuerdo Amanda	I remember you Amanda
la calle mojada	the wet street
corriendo a la fábrica	running to the factory
donde trabajaba Manuel.	where Manuel worked.
Con él	With him
que partió a la sierra	who took to the mountains
que nunca hizo daño	who never hurt anyone
que partió a la sierra	who took to the mountains
y en cinco minutos	and in five minutes
quedó destrozado	was wiped out
suena la sirena	the siren wails
de vuelta al trabajo	in returning to work
muchos no volvieron	many never returned
tampoco... Manuel	neither did…Manuel.
Te recuerdo Amanda	I remember you Amanda
corriendo a la fábrica	running to the factory
donde trabajaba Manuel.	where Manuel worked.

Every time that Robert had visited *Juan* and *Claudia*, he marveled at how a country as small as Chile, with its relatively small population, could produce such a rich variety and quality of folklore music. Social injustice had, almost overnight, yielded a series of stinging political songs that the powerful in the United States and Chile could not ignore. As his plane touched down at Miami airport, he realized that tears had been running down his cheeks for quite some time. He hoped that he could get back soon to Chile. He realized that there was an ache in his heart for *Rosa*!

Artemisa – (redrawn from Muñoz, 1959)

Chapter 11
A Dark Day
January, 1974

"Por la razón o la fuerza." (By reason or by force.) – part of the Chilean national anthem.

Rosa and her mother rose early that day. *Paulina* was still asleep in her crib. *Rosa's* mother quickly packed a lunch for *Rosa* and they both went out into the shed to fill a bag with oats for the horse. They said *"Chao,"* and *Rosa* started the long ride up into the mountains to see how the sheep were doing on the new summer forage.

Quinto wanted to come along but *Rosa* sent him back as she began to canter up the trail. This was the dog that *Roberto* had given her mother on that last day as he left the valley almost a year ago, and she had to admit that she missed him, even with his strange habits and customs. She laughed to herself and wondered if *Roberto* suspected that he had a daughter in Chile. *Quinto* sat there for a while and watched her go. Then, as he returned to the house, he saw the cars coming down the valley road.

The train of three cars, two black sedans and a military vehicle, turned off the main valley road and stopped at the turnoff to the *González* farm. After a few minutes, the military vehicle turned to the side by the gate, stopped, and three men got out. The other two cars drove up the side road and right up the main road to the main entrance at the back of the house. It was barely dawn and still rather chilly for a summer day. As two men got out of each car *Quinto* began to bark, growing more agitated the closer they got. The men walked toward the house, removing small machine guns from under their coats.

Inside the house, *Juan* and *Claudia* arose, glanced out of their upstairs window, and quickly donned their robes. *Juan* then said, *"¡Mi amor*, I think our destiny has arrived!"* *Claudia* responded, "Stall them

82

while I hide *Paulina*." Then she kissed him and took *Paulina* out of her crib and went toward the closet.

The men arrived at the house. One man shot the barking *Quinto* and went around to the front of the house. The other men stepped up to the main entrance at the back porch as the door opened. *Juan* stepped outside and exclaimed, "*¡Por Dios!* What is happening?" Then he saw *Quinto* thrashing around on the ground and yelping. "What do you want?" he asked, fear filling his voice. One of the men said, "We are here to put an end to your subversive socialist music." With that he shot *Juan*, spraying him across his chest with a half-dozen shots. *Juan* fell backward as if a mighty tree had fallen and hit the porch floor with a loud crash.

The two men burst into the house, shouting and turning over furniture. *Claudia* came down the stairs and screamed. One man shouted, "*Puta desgraciada, muere subversiva.*" They shot her in several sprays of bullets. The men left the bodies where they had fallen, then collected guitars and other musical instruments and some furniture, and piled the pieces and a few papers and rugs in a pile in the middle of the downstairs front room. They threw a kerosene lamp onto the pile and tried to start a fire, but at first it only smoldered with few flames.

One man shouted, "I see lights at the next ranch, I think someone is coming." Then they left in a roar of squealing tires and flying dirt. By the time the two sedans arrived at the turnoff, the military vehicle had already fled and was speeding down the road toward *Curacautín*.

Only halfway up the mountain road, *Rosa* barely heard the first staccato bursts of gunfire and could not imagine what they might mean. Then she felt a dark premonition and galloped back down the trail. As she rounded the last curve above the house, she saw three cars just leaving the turnoff to their road and turning onto the main road. She could not imagine what could have happened.

Then she saw smoke billowing up from the front side of the house. As she galloped closer, she saw *Quinto* thrashing around on the ground and yelping as if in great pain. Then she felt more than saw her father lying on the porch. She ran up to him but he was dead. *"¡Mamá!"* she cried and ran into the smoke-filled house. The pile of debris in the middle of the room was just starting to burn fiercely but she quickly pulled at the rug under the blazing mass and dragged most of the fire out into the yard.

She ran back into the house and, through the smoke she could see her mother lying on the floor in a growing pool of blood. From the magnitude of the wounds and the number of bullet holes she knew that she could do nothing for her. *"¡Paulina! Paulina!* Where are you?" *Rosa* stepped over her mother's body and ran upstairs into the bedroom. The baby crib was empty! *"¡Paulina, Paulina! ¿Dónde estás?"* Her quick scan over the room revealed nothing. She looked in the closet – nothing! Then she looked under the bed and saw *Paulina's* little hands wriggling above her blanket. *Rosa* pulled her out and could see no injury. She held the baby close to her chest and cried, "What will we do now, *Paulinita?"*

Her parents had heard rumors that the Pinochet regime did not like the old Chilean folk music and tried to discourage people from singing or listening to it. Had they done this? What insanity! She thought as tears filled her eyes and she sat down hard on the floor. She didn't know how long she sat there, but she slowly became aware of *Quinto's* yelping in the yard.

She held *Paulina* close to her and went out to see him. Although he was in obvious pain, his tail wagged when he saw her. He had chewed off the rest of his injured leg and was licking the stump. She knelt beside him and saw his hind leg lying on the ground. She tied a rag bandage around the stump and that seemed to sooth *Quinto* a lot. He then limped over and sniffed *Juan's* body and later went into the house and did the same at *Claudia's* body. Then he went over to *Paulina* and lay down beside her bed. He seemed to understand that the two adults were dead and he lay there looking at *Rosa*, wagging his tail each time she spoke to him or patted his head.

84

Soon, neighbors streamed into the yard and ran up to the house. Many asked, "What happened?" "Why?" "What had these poor people done to deserve this?" One voice in the crowd murmured, *"Así mataron a mi hijo en Santiago,* it was the *milicos."* (That's how they killed my son in *Santiago.* The military did it.)

Rosa handed *Paulina* to a neighbor and collapsed onto the ground, sobbing. "What would she do now? Her parents had been killed in a senseless act of violence. Thank goodness, *Miguel* was still safe in *Santiago.* But, *Roberto* was gone. Where was Vietnam? What would she do now?"

Litre - **LITHI** – (redrawn from Muñoz, 1959)

Chapter 12
Miguel
1974

"La Bala" (The bullet.) – Title of protest song written by *Víctor Jara.*

Miguel was a few years older than *Rosa*. He was born in 1945. As a young boy and teenager he sang folk songs with his family. His parents recognized him as an exceptionally smart young lad and, so, sent him to high school in *Temuco*. *Juan* had family members living there and they were happy to shelter *Miguel*. In his last year he transferred to a high school in *Santiago* and lived with another relative, at the same 2266 *San Alfonso* address where Jean and *Luisa* had stayed many years before.

Miguel was an active young man and had a part-time job working in a super market. Then, after he graduated, he worked for several years in one of the French-owned mines near *Santiago*. Robert had met *Miguel* only once, when he had visited his parents in *Lonquimay* and when Robert happened to be there working in his tent pressing plants.

While working in the mine *Miguel* had become an active member of the local mine workers union. Soon he began work with the government agency *CORFO*, which was responsible for developing policies to enhance economic development. *Miguel* was very much in favor of the *Allende* candidacy during the 1970s presidential campaign and worked hard in this new role. While working at *CORFO*, he married and soon he and his wife had two sons.

Because of his political leanings, and his former experience singing folk songs with his parents, he became a good friend of *Víctor Jara*, then a lector at the Technical University in *Santiago*. Their friendship became stronger when *Victor* learned that *Miguel's* parents were the ones who sang folk and protest songs.

It was with great exuberance and no small amount of trepidation that the *Allende* supporters entered the new presidential term. From the start, there was great opposition from the wealthy Chilean elite because they felt that their position of privilege in society was threatened. The end of the *Allende* presidency was assured, though, when the U. S. government became involved in promoting and funding civil and subversive activities. It started with secretly funding workers' strikes and any public demonstrations that weakened the *Allende* government. It worsened with the suspected involvement in several political assassinations, and it culminated in the not-so-secret efforts of Henry Kissinger and Richard Nixon to initiate a military coup against the *Allende* presidency.

After the coup on September 11, 1973, the situation rapidly spiraled downward. The military was quick to cleanse the country of any subversive individuals or organizations such as trade unions. Union members were among the first to be targeted and the military began to identify them. The spaghetti manufacturing factories of Lucchetti and Carozzi had strong unions. The factories were surrounded one day after the workers had started work. The doors were blocked shut and everyone inside was shot as they tried to escape.

Miguel was quick to see the emerging dangers and became a French citizen in early 1975, drawing on the fact that his grandfather had immigrated from France in 1920. He assumed that that would give him some degree of protection. He had a good, giving heart and helped many union members to escape from Chile, the main method being to get them into a foreign embassy that would give them protection.

Initially *Miguel* thought that the coup leaders would not harass a small fish like him, but several incidents occurred that made him begin to fear not only for his safety, but also for his life. On New Year's Day, 1974, he, his wife and their two small children, visited some distant relatives in *Conchalí*, a suburb on the north side of *Santiago*. Prior to that, the military had decreed that there could be no gatherings of more than 5 people. A distant cousin of *Miguel's* wife was visiting from the United States, with her 4-year-old daughter. Chileans are, of course, gregarious and extremely friendly, so a get-together was planned so that all the cousins, friends, and neighbors could have a chance to visit the visiting mother and her infant daughter.

Sometime between 9:00 AM and lunch, several dozen individuals had stopped by to offer their greetings. Everyone was aware of the crowd rule so greetings were short and to the point, leaving a core of perhaps 13 or so, visitors on the property in various stages of coming or going. The table was set up outside under the grape arbor and loaded with food and drink.

Suddenly the roar of a small airplane was heard above the conversation. It circled over the house at a low altitude and on one of its over-flights, a cloudy material was released. As the cloud drifted down to the ground, a strong odor of gasoline was noted, and it fell on the food and the plants in the patio. The food had to be discarded and several days later most of the plants were either visibly injured or had died of chemical poisoning. Of course, this broke up the festivities.

Several days later, the outraged, and fearful, victims were invited to a small get-together on the beach near the village of *El Quisco*, on the Pacific coast. Approximately 8 individuals were gathered on the beach and engaged in conversation when a small airplane flew over and then circled around above the group at extremely low altitude, as if taking photographs. Of course, this broke up the gathering and all scurried back to their automobiles and left.

These experiences, and others, had a profound effect on those affected and made them afraid, or even terrified, which was exactly the effect that the military wanted. *Miguel* returned to *Santiago* and began to realize that he must leave Chile before he was killed.

Miguel was quite ingenious, though, and while he prepared to leave Chile, continued with his schemes to get refugees past the police

88

and into either the Italian or French embassies. Once he pushed a refugee dressed as a nun seated in a wheelchair into the Italian embassy. But word soon got around that the police knew who he was and were actively seeking him. So, *Miguel* left Chile late in 1974. His wife drove him to the bus station and he took a bus to *Mendoza*, Argentina. He wanted his wife and two sons to go with him but she chose not to go. How he escaped is rather miraculous but the situation was still rather chaotic and he somehow slipped through the cracks.

And, for a while, the cracks were pretty large. The military tried to force the *Carabineros* to help with domestic obligations but many *Carabineros* were not sympathetic to the ideals of the coup. They could not realistically resist the well-armed military. Most of the street police were only armed with .32 caliber revolvers and carried only a few bullets.

So, many decent and honest policemen did what they could to help the population at large. They tried to not be as zealous as the military in enforcing the new laws. The public, of course, knew this and coined the term *"Sandías"*, meaning that they were red on the inside but green on the outside, green being the color of their uniforms. This is the opposite of what one might suspect but Chileans can be very sarcastic in their humor and everyone knew what this term meant. In fact, many *Carabineros* served as a buffer between the military and the public, especially those directly affected by the military's actions. They served a very valuable function in relaying rumors and news of dead or disappeared individuals to their relatives and loved ones.

A friend of *Miguel's*, *Don Humberto Soto*, had friends in *Mendoza* and they helped *Miguel* get a fresh start. He had taken some savings with him with which he purchased a small bar. But, when *Miguel* heard that the Chilean secret police were looking for him, he began drinking. He sold the bar and fled to northern Brazil where his friends said he might find refuge. They sent him to the small city of *Boa Vista*. He spent a few days looking for a contact, an elderly man of European extraction who owned a dairy farm.

Miguel worked for him for a while and they got along very well, becoming good friends. *Miguel* told his friend that he wanted to bring his wife and sons to live with him, but that his wife was not willing to leave Chile until he had a secure job and a safe future. So, they made plans to build a yogurt plant. At last it looked as though *Miguel* was going to do well and could build a prosperous future for his family.

Neither *Miguel* nor his Brazilian friend could have foreseen the extent to which the Chilean military would go to find and punish any one they considered as subversive. This is why Operation *Cóndor* came into being.

At least once a month *Miguel* would call his relatives in *Santiago* and they would relay his messages to his parents in *Lonquimay*. On one of the calls he learned that his parents had been killed. In 1976 or 1977 his calls ceased altogether. No one had any idea what might have happened. Several months later, a *Carabinero* stopped by the former house of *Juan* and *Claudia* and told *Rosa* what little he had been able to find out about the fate of *Miguel*.

The *Carabineros* in *Lonquimay* and *Curacautín* had been good friends of the *González* family for many years. When the military coup occurred in 1973, the *Carabineros* in general had not been very sympathetic to the military nor the coup. Most *Carabineros* stationed in the countryside or in small towns had come to know and respect their neighbors. They were not about to cooperate in a blood bath. So, one way in which they could still serve the community would be to milk the military authorities for whatever information they could and then pass it along to victims' families.

What they had learned was that *DINA* operatives had traced *Miguel's* whereabouts and finally discovered that he was working at the dairy farm. When *DINA* operatives had begun asking around about him in *Boa Vista*, friends had gotten word to him about their questions. *DINA* had several teams involved in tracking down and killing people. Usually, a first group would locate the person of interest, and then a second, or third, group would move in and dispatch the victim. Every

90

step was carefully planned so as to be secretive, yet make sure that they eliminated their target.

Miguel quickly packed some clothes and what little money he had and ran out the back door, into the surrounding forest and back into town. He purchased a bus ticket to Venezuela and left with only what he was carrying. Apparently he was already under surveillance because when he got off the bus in Venezuela another group of operatives was waiting for him. As they approached, *Miguel* bolted and ran into the surrounding forest.

The operatives chased him and never even requested that he surrender. As soon as they chased him deep into the forest, they shot him point blank in the back, robbed him, and then dumped his body into the *Orinoco* River. As dozens of *piraña* fish swarmed around *Miguel's* body, the assassins knew that he would never be found. *Miguel* was never seen nor heard from again, leaving a widow and two small children, and he joined the ranks of *los desaparecidos*.

The tragedy of *Miguel*, and that of his parents, was experienced several thousands of times in the first few years during and after the military coup, causing immeasurable grief to their families. And for no reason except to show how bestial the human spirit can be!

Where are the disappeared? (redrawn from portion of a
photograph in *Meiselas*, 1990)

Chapter 13
A Letter to *Rosa*
April, 1974

"Mantelito blanco." (The white tablecloth.)– Title of song from Chilean folklore.

Several months after the death of her parents, *Rosa* was clearing out some of their clothes and other personal belongings. In her mother's old trunk she found her grandmother's *mantelito blanco* wrapped around a bark-covered package, wrapped in the manner of the old *Pehuenche* documents she had seen occasionally as a child at her grandmother's house.

The *mantelito blanco* was from her great-grandmother who said it was made from the finest linen in France during the 1700s. It was a precious family heirloom. Inside the bark-covered parcel there was a letter, addressed to *Rosa*, from her mother! She unfolded it with shaking hands and began to sob. After a few minutes, she was able to begin reading it.

The letter read as follows: '*Rosa*, my dear, dear *Rosa*, I have loved you more than anything you can know and share with you the deep, deep sorrow you are feeling now. Several months ago, about the time of the military coup, I had a premonition that your father and I will soon die. Within that premonition your brother *Miguel* also faces an uncertain future.'

Rosa had to sit down and she cried for a while. Then she continued reading. '*Rosa*, as you know, I am a *Pehuenche* **machi**, just as my grandmother and my mother were before me. We have certain powers. The powers are small at first, but they grow more powerful as we grow older. We can't make the dead rise or anything like that but we are able to do certain simpler things. For one thing we can see into some of the future. I see that someday you will also be a **machi**, and

92

you will understand how we feel, and know what are your responsibilities, to your family, and to the community.'

'*Rosa*, you must not repel *Roberto*. I know that he will father your child. He is a good young man. Eventually he will fall in love with you and you will have a good life together. Soon he will save my life and much later he will try to save your life. I can't see the details, but I feel in my heart what the future brings. The two of you have much to give our *Pehuenche* community. Know that I will always be with you as far as I am able. I will try to send signs. At first you will not recognize the signs, but it is vital that *Roberto* study and analyze them. Remember also that every time you see one of these signs, you will know that I am near to you and your family. I bless you, your mother, *Claudia*.'

Rosa sat there on the floor, too stunned to move for a long time. 'Soon he will save my life!' She re-read that phrase. "How can that be?" *Rosa* was confused. Then she remembered seeing him jump into the river to save her mother's life, only a little over a year ago, but how could her mother have known that was going to happen? And her mother had written this letter to her even before then! Just then, a breath of wind blew a cluster of leaves against the bedroom window, and *Rosa* shuddered, cried again, and said,"*Mamá, Mamá*, why did you have to leave me, what will I do now?"

But, *Roberto* was gone, gone to Vietnam as a soldier, and during the past year she had lost contact with him. He was in the field and isolated from communications. Then she cried again as she felt the terrible loneliness in her heart. What was she going to do now? *Roberto* didn't even know that she had become pregnant with his baby. She couldn't return to the university, even if she could afford to go.

She had to take care of the little ranch and her baby and must help *Miguel* as best as she could. Her parents had a little money hidden away but it would not last long. She would have to increase the sheep and cattle herds and hire some help for the animals. The military would certainly never allow her to sing again even if they allowed her to

93

live. She felt terribly alone, even though occasional gusts of wind blew leaves against the window, and even though she suspected that it was a sign from her mother.

Boldo – (redrawn from *Muñoz*, 1959)

Chapter 14
Vietnam Highlands
1974

As the patrol worked its way down into the little valley, each man knew that they were walking into an extremely dangerous situation. The valley, more of a wide ravine actually, was surrounded by rich paddies, and broken into narrow, shallow ravines. This was not the more typical well-defined rice growing area in the delta where the paddies were large and separated by narrow walkways. Here the visibility was not so good as there were scattered lines of trees in the ravines and along the watercourses, but there were only a few workers in the paddies and there didn't seem to be a trace of Viet-Cong.

As the patrol moved into a small woodlot, or copse, Robert could see through it to the clearing a little further down the ravine. A small cluster of Vietnamese peasants was working there. As the last man entered the copse, shots started to ring out. Viet-Cong! As each man sought shelter, the firing quickly became so intense that the quantity of bits of leaves and twigs falling made it seem like snowflakes were falling around them.

Robert threw himself down behind a slight rise and wriggled out of his pack and then pushed it in front of him on the rise. The soldier next to him was struggling to remove his pack and Robert rolled over to help him. Just as Robert removed the pack, the man slowly rolled toward him and Robert saw the bullet hole in his forehead and a single drop of blood trickling down his face.

The patrol leader was shouting commands and there was the beginning of a little return fire. Robert could clearly hear the tweets of whistles as the Viet-Cong officers issued commands to their soldiers. As Robert began to assess the situation, he looked toward the rim of the little ravine and his heart fell as he could see a line of white pith

95

helmets moving around the ravine edge! There were dozens, if not more, and that was only in the direction that was visible to him.

Now the firing was becoming more intense as the Viet-Cong moved into their positions, and large chunks of bark and tree limbs began raining down on the patrol. The men were firing desperately but it was becoming very clear to every man that they were badly outnumbered and would likely die there before day's end. Their firing slowed a little as they tried to conserve ammunition. The radioman had been hit and the radio smashed by the same bullet. Robert pulled out half of his full ammunition clips and re-arranged them on the ground in front of him so he could reload more quickly. He knew they weren't going anywhere because there was no place to go except closer to the Viet-Cong. They must really be enjoying this! Not a good situation for us!

As he began to control his excitement and his firing, he tried to overview their situation. He noticed that further down in the ravine the little cluster of peasants was huddled together and screaming. The Viet-Cong were not firing at them, though. Every few minutes he could hear a scream from one of the men in his patrol as the withering fire from the Viet-Cong hit their target. By now, though, the ring of Viet-Cong had completely surrounded the little ravine, putting the peasants right in the center of fire from both adversaries, and he knew that it was only a matter of time before they would be killed by stray bullets.

He rolled over on his back and slid down a little for more cover and to think a little more about what was happening. As he glanced behind him he noticed a figure standing off about 30 yards in front of the ravine edge. It seemed to be a woman dressed in some kind of strange dress he had not seen since he had left Chile and her feet were not touching the ground.

Fascinated, he forgot about the firing and as he stared at the figure he thought he could hear the figure speak to him, "Robert, you must help them as you helped me." Robert thought to himself, "What kind of crap is this? Am I finally losing my mind?" The figure then repeated the request, this time in Spanish, *"Roberto, ayúdales como tú me ayudaste."* "Help them like you helped me!"

Robert thought he was going into shock! It looked like *Claudia*, *Rosa's* mother whom he had pulled from the river in Chile a year earlier! This was impossible! As he heard more screams from his men, he thought, "This can't be! I must be cracking up from the situation." Now she was pleading with her arms and repeating her request. Almost without thinking, he wriggled out of his belts and other paraphernalia and threw them down along side his pack on the low ridge in front of him. As he stood up he heard some of his mates say, "Robert, get down, are you fucking crazy?"

As he ran down the slope toward the peasants, he thought he must indeed be crazy. Bullets clipped off bits of his uniform but none touched him. He thought to himself, "Boy, I am so dead!" When he neared the group of peasants he saw that the only ones still alive were a skinny old man, a skinny young woman, and a baby. Without hesitating a second, he grabbed the old man and woman together and threw them over his shoulder. He then picked up the baby and cradled it in his arms. He turned around and began to run as fast as he could, staggering all the way with a mass of legs and arms sticking out in all directions. When he got back to his patrol, he jumped in headfirst and fell into a clump of arms, legs, and the woman's long black hair. In a flashback he remembered *Rosa's* long, black hair.

As his men pulled the Vietnamese peasants off him, he looked over to the figure and heard her say, *"Bien hecho, m'ijito.* Now you must save *Rosa's* sanity, and yours. Well done my son." Then her image disappeared and Robert wondered what he had just seen, or imagined he had seen. One of the men stepped up beside him, slapped him on the back and said, "Robert, we thought your ass was grass. Why did you do that? You must be fucking crazy!"

All Robert could realize was that he was still alive and hadn't even been hit! And, the silence – the firing had stopped! He heard a faint tweeting and someone said that the Viet-Cong were leaving. Were they leaving out of respect for what he had done? They certainly weren't afraid of his small patrol. He was grateful for having survived the ordeal! But, what had just happened?

Robert was nearing the end of his one-year tour of duty in Vietnam when he was wounded. It happened several weeks after he was given new orders. After his patrol returned to the base and word got around about what he had done, his base commander was afraid that he might be mentally unstable and decided to change his assignment to something, perhaps, a little safer.

Because of Robert's past experience as a smokejumper he thought he would feel comfortable serving as an aerial artillery spotter. So, Robert was re-assigned to the Da Nang airbase and spent several months as an artillery spotter flying in a small two-place airplane. He and the pilot would fly around possible Vietnam troop concentrations and call in artillery fire to the best effect.

Sometimes they would fly around a crash site and direct artillery fire around the site as Vietnam soldiers surrounded the site looking for the pilot and/or his crew. He knew they knew they were there because the forest would literally twinkle as rifle fire from the ground was aimed at their plane. Usually they were too high to be hit but frequently, after they returned to the base, the many bullet holes in the plane had to be patched.

On one mission, the plane was hit by ground fire and the pilot lost control. As the plane dropped lower and lower the pilot tried to land in a river. But the plane crashed into the river and flipped over. As the plane struck the water, Robert saw the pilot's head snap back and forth. Robert struck the side of the plane and was momentarily knocked out. When he came to, the plane was filling with water and Robert knew he had to get out, fast.

He cut himself out of the seat harness and pushed out the hinged window. He somehow forced himself out and into the water. He swam to shore and climbed up the bank and hid in the thick

98

undergrowth while he caught his breath. He saw a few bubbles surface where the plane had rapidly sunk. The pilot did not surface, and Robert knew that he was dead.

Robert pulled out his revolver and checked to see that it was loaded. Then he scrunched down into the undergrowth as he heard the noise of a motorboat coming up the river. He strained to see through the brush as the boat moved past and was disappointed to see that it was a Viet-Cong boat. It slowed opposite his hiding place and then trolled back and forth as the crew searched for any evidence of the wreck or survivors. He could see the crew gesture with their arms as they were apparently discussing whether they should go ashore. Finally the boat turned back into the current and speeded up as it moved away.

It was now near dusk. Robert hid in the same dense thicket all night, holding his revolver in front of him in case the Viet-Cong returned and he needed to defend himself. With first daylight he inventoried his belongings and began to ponder what he might do next. He had no supplies, other than 12 extra bullets for his revolver. His water and emergency food rations had sunk with the plane. He decided to not drink from the river yet, as he decided to head east, to where his last look at the map had indicated approximately where the U. S. lines were.

Robert stayed hidden during that day and traveled toward the east at night. On the morning of the third day after the crash, he heard several Huey helicopters flying toward his general direction. For the last several hours he had sensed that some Viet-Cong were tracking him. He was afraid that they would soon catch him. So, when he saw that the choppers were going to fly almost directly over his location, he decided to take a chance and jumped up, waving his shirt, trying to get the pilot's attention. The Viet-Cong were now close behind and when they saw the first chopper turn and begin to circle Robert, they quickly set up a mortar and began to lob rounds at him. The Viet-Cong were very good with mortar fire.

As the chopper circled again in preparation to land, its gunner sprayed the Viet-Cong with machine gun fire. But, even as the gunner fired, a mortar round was already in the air. As the chopper circled again, the last mortar round exploded a yard from where Robert was standing. The explosion lifted him several yards in the air and threw him about twelve feet or so off to one side.

At first Robert felt no pain. His only thought, as he flew through the air and saw a leg slowly rotating away from him, that some poor dumb schnock had just lost a leg. He fell hard to the ground, but still felt no pain. His last memory as he passed out was of an American medic crouching over him and beginning to administer first aid. Then, he entered into a coma that would last a long time.

Ortiga – (redrawn from *Muñoz*, 1959)

Chapter 15
The World Turned Upside Down
1974

St. Patrick's Hospital, Missoula, Montana – July, 1980.

Robert's mother came to the hospital that morning, just as she or her husband had each day for the past 6 years. Robert had been in a coma since the day a mortar blast had blown off his left leg just below the knee. The shock of the explosion had traumatized his brain in such a way that he had gone into a deep coma, and no amount of treatment had yet brought him back successfully into consciousness.

He had first been treated at the VA hospital in Great Falls but since his coma had remained and it appeared that he might never again regain consciousness, he was sent to St. Patrick's Hospital in Missoula. They had started a large and aggressive physical therapy program there and since he would be closer to his parents, it was felt that it would be less of a strain on them if he was closer to where they lived, and the aggressive program would help him retain some of his muscle tone.

Year after year went by, with little sign of improvement. Robert remained in a deep coma. One day a group of student nurses visiting from Chile stopped at St. Patrick's Hospital to study the hospital's physical therapy techniques. They were told about Robert, that he had worked in Chile, and how long he had been in a coma. When they were shown the physical therapy techniques being used on him, they spontaneously burst into song, in Spanish! After singing a short medley of Chilean folk songs, they moved on to the next patient. As they were leaving, one of the therapists glanced at Robert as she passed by his bed, and thought she noticed a tear in his eye.

After that day, Robert's parents brought in a portable record player and twice a week when Robert's mother brought fresh flowers for his room she, or her husband, would remain at Robert's side for several hours, either reading aloud to him, or sitting there with him listening to Chilean music, with long-dried tears on their grieving faces.

Today, Robert's mother was especially jubilant, carrying a small vase of branchlets of **Chilco** (*fuchsia*) plants with her to place in Robert's room. She knew that he would especially appreciate them if he could see them. He had sent her seeds of this plant years ago when he was collecting medicinal plants in Chile and she knew that he would be particularly pleased, as he had loved his work in Chile. Not only were *fuchsia* plants valuable as medicinals, they also produced unique and beautiful flowers.

As she approached his room she thought she heard voices from within. Not wanting to interrupt in case the nurses were discussing something of a private nature, she hesitated outside the partially open door and listened. She heard what seemed to be a young lady imploring something to someone in the room.

Drawing upon her high school Spanish, she thought the voice said something like, '*Por favor, Roberto, tú tienes que ayudar a Rosa. Ella necesita tu ayuda. Por favor, anda donde ella.*' (Please, Robert, you must help *Rosa*. She needs your help. Please go to her.) Then she heard a weak voice that she recognized as Robert's, "*Claudia*, you look so young, what has happened to you? What has happened to *Rosa*?"

Robert's mother dropped the vase and it smashed on the floor. She ran back to the nurse's station screaming, "Robert is awake and he is speaking!" The nurses and an on-duty doctor ran to Robert's room, burst through the door and immediately began taking readings from the various instruments attached to Robert. Robert's mother followed them and said to Robert, "Thank God you are awake. Robert do you feel alright?" Robert weakly raised a hand toward her and said, "Mom, I think I'm going to be okay."

She called her husband and told him what had happened and while waiting for him she went back to Robert's room and asked, "Robert what happened to the young lady who you were speaking with before I entered the room? Where had she gone so quickly before the

102

nurses came and how had she left the room without being seen? She was speaking to you in Spanish with so much vigor and passion."

Robert waited for a long moment before answering, "Mom, I honestly don't know. But, I think that was *Claudia*, a middle-aged lady I met in Chile. Yet, now she appeared to me as if she was only barely in her early twenties. She told me that her daughter, *Rosa*, was in some kind of trouble and needed my help. As I recall, I think she also appeared to me when I was in the coma but I couldn't answer her, I could only hear her. When I was in Vietnam, she also appeared to me, but as the middle-aged lady that I knew in Chile and asked me to help some Vietnamese peasants who were in danger of being killed."

They continued talking for quite some time. By this time Robert's father had arrived and the three of them hugged each other and mingled many tears of joy for the fact that Robert had finally emerged from his coma. After much conversation to catch up on what had happened during the last six years, Robert announced that he was going to work hard on his physical therapy, as he had to go back to Chile to see what he could do to help *Rosa*.

He told his parents who she was and when they saw the firmness in his eyes and voice, and they sensed the love that he felt for her, they looked at each other and even though they didn't want him to go, agreed that this would be the best thing that he could do to help with his rehabilitation.

When the nurses finally came in that evening and began to shoo out Robert's parents, Robert's mother noticed that the vase of *fuchsia* flowers that had fallen to the floor when she dropped it, was now standing on the nightstand, and that the vase, which she had seen shatter, was holding the flowers and was not broken. She never told anyone what she had seen, but she pondered what it meant.

Chilco – (redrawn from *Muñoz*, 1959)

Chapter 16
Back in Chile
November, 1980

¡Pucha que es linda mi tierra! – Verse of song from Chilean folklore

Robert and *Rosa* just lay there on the bare ground, hugging each other, not believing what had just happened and that they were finally together again! Their eyes were filled with tears and both were sobbing. After awhile *Paulina* came up to them and started to both laugh and cry at the same time.

Then she began to kick Robert and scolded him, *"¿Tú, huevón desgraciado, por qúe dejaste a mi mamá sola? ¿Por qúe me dejaste a mi sola?"* (Disgraceful one with large testicles, why did you desert my mother? Why did you desert me?) Then, she too began to sob and crawled into Robert's lap and hugged him. *Rosa* said, *"M'ijita."* Then both she and Robert held *Paulina* tightly in their arms.

Mother and daughter gazed into Robert's eyes as he asked, "Where are your parents? This place looks as if it hasn't had much care for quite awhile." *Rosa* answered, "They are both dead, *Roberto*, killed by the military for singing their so-called subversive music. We think *Miguel* is dead too, becaue we haven't heard from him or seen his body. We only have the word of a business partner in Brazil that the *DINA* police were asking about him, and then he just disappeared! Another rumor had placed him in Venezuela, where he was said to have been killed. We just don't know. He has never contacted his wife or me. He has simply disappeared!"

After awhile *Rosa* invited Robert into the house to have tea. As she prepared tea, she explained about the charcoal spot on the ceiling and how the house almost burned down the day her parents were killed. She said she had tried to clean up everything as best as she could. She told him about the terror, which soon turned to grief, that she felt when she saw her dead parents. She related how *Quinto* had been shot in the leg and that she had to trim the stump and then bandage him, and that he had recovered quite well, and that he was a good companion for her and *Paulina*. Then she suddenly became silent. She brought in the tea and cookies and invited *Roberto* and *Paulina* to sit. She poured tea for herself and then sat down.

Robert then said, "You know, when I was in that dark place during the coma, one of the things I remember distinctly was the Chilean folklore music. I swear that I heard song after song that you and your parents played for me during my visits here. *Rosa* looked at him with her large eyes and then left her place at the table and disappeared upstairs. When she came back down she was carrying a guitar and said to Robert, "This is the only musical instrument the *milicos* didn't destroy. I have so missed playing it. I simply did not have the desire to play music any more after my parents were killed and you were gone. But, my dear *Roberto*, this song I play gladly for you."

Then she played the guitar and sang to him this song from Chilean folklore:

Si vas para Chile	(If you go to *Chile*)
te ruego que pases	(I demand that you go)
por donde vive mi amada.	(to where my love lives.)
Es una casita	(It is a tiny house)
muy linda y chiquita,	(very pretty and tiny,)
que esta en la falda	(it's in the shadow)
de un cerro enclavada.	(of a nearby mountain.)
La adornan las parras,	(Grapevines decorate it,)
la cruza un estero:	(a brook crosses it,)
y al frente hay un sauce	(and in the front there is a willow tree)
que llora, que llora,	(that weeps, that weeps,)
porque yo la quiero.	(because I love her.)
Si vas para Chile	(If you go to Chile)

te ruego, viajero,	(I demand, traveler,)
le digas a ella que	(you tell her that)
de amor me muero.	(of that love for her I die.)

During the next few hours, *Rosa* and Robert talked constantly, she sharing with him more details of the brutal killing of her family, he told her about his experiences in Vietnam, of having seen and heard *Claudia* urging him to save the lives of the Vietnamese family, and then seeing a much younger *Claudia* when in the coma, urging him to help *Rosa*. Robert teased *Paulina* and played with her and *Quinto*, often just doing silly things that they could share with each other.

They became accustomed to each other and fell in love again, and Robert began to get to know the daughter he never knew he had. *Rosa* showed Robert the letter that her mother had left for her. They discussed what it might mean, but they had to admit that *Claudia* had correctly predicted her and *Juan's* demise and that *Miguel* faced an uncertain future. *Miguel* had disappeared in 1974, shortly after their parents were killed by the Pinochet regime, and rumors had speculated that he had fled Chile and spent several months and perhaps years fleeing DINA, the Chilean Secret Police.

Rosa also told him about the murder of a cousin of her mother. *Jaime Guzmán Aldunate* was a lawyer who lived in *Santiago*. From one of *Santiago's* leading families, he had vigorously defended copper miners during several of their strikes during the *Allende* regime. He disappeared. Several weeks later, one of the neighborhood *Carabineros* stopped by the house and told his widow that he had been killed and his body was in the general cemetery in *Viña del Mar*. So, she hired a cab to take her from *Santiago* to *Viña*, which is a distance of over 40 miles, to the general cemetery there.

Upon her arrival, the soldier guarding the cemetery would not let her in. Finally, after much crying and pleading he let her in and led her to a pile of perhaps several dozen naked bodies. The soldier helped her examine the bodies until finally she found her husband. His throat had been slit from ear to ear and from the numerous bruises on his body, it was evident that he had been tortured. By this time the soldier was crying as well. He helped her load the body into the cab and she returned to *Santiago*. He had left a widow and two children. After that time his wife was never really normal again and she slipped deeper and deeper into insanity as she grew older.

That evening, when the three of them were seated at the supper table and having a rather sparse bite to eat, Robert asked *Rosa*, "How were you able to get by? You obviously don't have much money. How did you and *Paulina* survive all these years? Why didn't you marry?"

Rosa replied, "*Roberto*, we have almost starved to death. My parents left hidden a little money but it has been stretched very thin. We sell a few sheep and cattle and have maintained a small garden. *Gracias a Díos* to the people of *Lonquimay*! They supported us to a large extent all this time. They loved my parents, and my grandparents as well, and have tried to repay all that my ancestors have done for them over the years. But, they are poor too and could not give much.

But, *Roberto*, my mother appeared to me in my dreams and said you would come, but that you were badly hurt. That is what kept me and *Paulina* going. I loved you *Roberto* and I knew that you would come someday, if you could."

Robert arose and went over to the chair where *Paulina* was seated. He bent down on one knee in front of her and said, "*Paulina*, you are a beautiful young lady. Today I found out that you are my daughter. I left your mother long ago. I don't how I could have been so stupid as to abandon such a beautiful young daughter, and her beautiful mother, both of whom I have come to love very much. "

"*Paulina*, if you and your mother will let me come back into your life, I promise that I will never leave you alone again, as long as I live." He turned toward *Rosa*, "*Rosa*, if you will be my wife I will try to be a good husband to you and a good father to this little urchin."

"When I was in the coma," he continued, "your mother came and spoke to me and said that you were in terrible straits and needed my help. The day I awoke from the coma, my mother also heard your mother speaking to me in my hospital room. *Rosa*, your mother had the face, body, and voice of a young woman! And I swear that I will never leave you again. I will try to make up for my absence. If you and *Paulina* will have me, I have found a great treasure here in Chile and I will stay with you, and take care of you, as long as I live." Then he stood up.

Paulina also stood up, looked him square in the eyes, kicked him once hard in the shin of his good leg, and then jumped into his arms and began crying. *Rosa* came over to the two of them, hugged them both tightly and replied, "*Roberto*, oh, yes, yes, yes! I have loved you since that first day I saw you camped down by the river. Such a bashful, humble, young man! When you were a little tipsy you accidently touched me and turned beet red of embarrassment."

"What a nerdy young man! Mom was afraid that you were never going to follow your heart and pursue me. Maybe that is why she encouraged me to take you to that *canelo* grove on the mountain on the day before you were to have left Chile, and that's why she gave me the **Pilqui** to give you. Maybe she also knew in her heart how both of us felt toward each other and that was why she appeared to you first in Vietnam and then later in the hospital. She must have been watching over you just as she was watching over me and *Paulina*."

At any rate, Robert had a new home, and a new family. He settled in pretty quickly, helping make repairs to the house while *Rosa* worked with the sheep and cattle herds. They discussed what their future might be and decided to sell the livestock but maintain a large garden. *Rosa* wanted to pursue her apprenticeship as a **machi** so she could better serve the communities of *Lonquimay* and *Curacautín*.

Robert had an idea that perhaps they could also work to form a cooperative to help market and sell native handicrafts as well as prepared medicinal plants. Robert's partners at Pharmtec offered financial assistance that had been postponed when *Claudia* and *Juan* were murdered. With that money they built a small office/museum in *Lonquimay* to serve as a headquarters for the cooperative.

At about that time in Chile, tourism began to become quite popular, especially from neighboring Argentina but increasingly from the United States and Europe and their business began to do quite well. It was an increasing asset for the community. Ever since the Chilean government nationalized the valley in the late 1800's, the living standards of the natives, by modern criteria, had not been good.

Since the *Pehuenches* had historically always been pretty much self-sufficient, they usually had enough to eat and could cloth themselves, but the increased availability of material goods such as automobiles, televisions, etc. were luxuries that most could not afford. Certainly, as the economy improved, life got a little better and by the late 1980's various government programs and better roads resulted in a much better standard of living for all.

Vuinque – (redrawn from *Muñoz*, 1959)

Chapter 17
Santa Teresa Church, *Lonquimay*
December, 1980

The little church was filled with people, and many more were standing outside in the beautiful early summer day. There was a feeling of great festivity in the air! A bride and groom, both simply dressed, were standing before the priest, both with radiant smiles on their faces. In fact, all the parishioners were smiling and the festivity of the occasion would have been highly contagious to any visitor on that day.

Robert's parents were there, escorted to the front row by *Paulina*. They had flown to Chile a week earlier from Missoula and had since been special guests of Robert and *Rosa*. They loved *Rosa* and *Paulina*, and the Araucaria pine forests surrounding the *Lonquimay* Valley. Robert, *Rosa*, and *Paulina* had met them at the airport in *Santiago* and his parents were quick to understand why Robert had been so anxious to return to Chile after he awoke from his coma.

After the service got underway, the priest began his homily, "Dearly beloved. We are gathered here today to join together this man and this woman in holy matrimony. Normally the Sacrament of Holy Matrimony is a rather short service. But I am going to depart slightly from this tradition by saying a few words, so that we can all share in the joy of this day."

"We all know this woman, *Rosa González*. I dare say that there is not a person in *Lonquimay* who does not know *Rosa González*. Her grandparents were stalwart citizens in this valley. We all knew her wonderful parents, and we have suffered with her during these last years as she raised her daughter alone in the world after the murder of her parents."

111

"With help from all the *Lonquimay* community, she survived, and raised a beautiful daughter. During this time, she had many suitors, some undoubtedly only trying to be of help, but certainly others who had developed a real affection for her and her daughter. But, *Rosa* had a great faith and she knew that one day her only true love would return, return from a far-off country, and from a far-off war where he was severely wounded."

"We all urged her to move on, to leave the pains of the past, forget the man she thought she loved and hoped would return. But, if anything, *Rosa* is stubborn. And she struggled to survive, managing her parents' farm as best as she could, and raising a few sheep."

"All of us here today know that her faith has been fulfilled, her *Roberto* has returned! Most of us didn't know *Roberto* very well. We knew him mostly as a shy young man, interested only in learning about medicinal plants. We have been told that he did not initially have any affection for *Rosa*."

"However, we learned a great deal about *Roberto* on that day in 1973 when *Claudia*, *Rosa's* mother, fell into the river and was drowning. We learned a great deal about *Roberto's* character when the rescue party finally arrived at the river and found him in the chillingly cold water. We saw him hanging onto a submerged branch with one hand and with the other holding *Claudia's* face out of the water so that she might not drown."

"He had hung on like this for over an hour while *Rosa* went frantically seeking assistance! When his rescuers dragged him out of the water, still holding onto *Claudia*, the only remark he made was, 'Take your time but hurry up."

"Then he collapsed and spent the next several days with a fever and severe chills. We know that only a few days later he left for the United States and went into military service and spent some time in Vietnam, was wounded, and then spent several years in a coma, suffering from his wounds."

112

"We welcome the parents of *Roberto* with open hearts and we know that they are impressed with their new daughter, and a beautiful granddaughter that they didn't know they had."

"And so, *Roberto* and *Rosa*, it is with great pride and joy that today I pronounce you to be husband and wife. *Roberto*, you may kiss your bride, and *Paulina*, don't watch your parents as they kiss."

After the wedding, Robert, *Rosa* and *Paulina* entertained Robert's parents. His parents fell in love with *Rosa* and especially *Paulina*. She was such a mature young lady. They all took a tour of southern Chile, from *Temuco* down south to *Puerto Montt* and even to the island of *Chiloe*. Robert showed them where he had collected medicinal plants and something about the history of the area. *Rosa* took along her guitar and sang many folklore songs. Robert's parents even picked up a little Spanish during their visit.

About a month after Robert's parents had returned to the States, Robert, *Rosa* and *Paulina* were eating lunch in their house when there was a knock on the door. Robert went to answer the knock and there stood the mail deliveryman with a special delivery letter that needed a signature. Robert said he could sign it but the mailman said, "No, it must be signed by the recipient, a *Señorita Paulina*."

After signing for the envelope, *Paulina* opened it and began to read the short message, "*Nuestra querida Paulina*" but then she stopped and said, "*Mamá, Papá*, the rest is in English." So Robert took the letter and read, "*Nuestra querida Paulina*, you know what that means don't you *Paulina*?" "Of course *Papá*, but what does the rest say?"

Robert continued, "During our all too short a visit with our son and his lovely wife, and especially their beautiful daughter, we have come to realize that we have a treasure in all of you. We shall plan to visit you often and hope you come to visit us often as well. *Paulina*, you are an intelligent young lady, so, we have placed a small amount of money in a bank account for you and your education. We love you and want only the best for you. Love, *los abuelitos*."

113

As *Paulina* examined the letter, something fell out of the envelope. It looked a little like a Chilean *carnet*, or identity card. But it was a bank passbook from the First National Bank of Missoula, Montana. Inside was a deposit made out to *Paulina* for the amount of $100,000. Robert and *Rosa* were stunned! Then they smiled as they realized that the expenses for *Paulina's* undergraduate education were covered.

Limpia Plata – **KELTRI LAWEN** (redrawn
from *Muñoz*, 1959)

Chapter 18
The Fire of 1983

"It was a skin bubbler." - Smokejumper jargon to describe an
extremely hot and fast burning fire.

This chapter is about a forest fire, a particular forest fire in the
Lonquimay Valley. The danger of a potentially devastating forest fire in
the area was always present but no major one had ever occurred during
the memory of even the oldest residents. This is partially because the
Pehuenche residents of the region were particularly careful with the use of
fire in the wild. And, most of the Araucaria pine stands were nearly
pure in species composition, all trees were of the same relative age (very
old), and with trunks of large diameter and dense crowns that limited
light penetration to the forest floor. This resulted in a rather sparse
growth of understory shrubs and other plants.

In order for a forest fire to start and then spread, several
factors must be present. Firstly, there must be a sufficient quantity of
fuels, these are the organic materials that combust, or burn, if the
temperature is sufficiently elevated. Fuels include the stems, branches,
and bark of standing trees, and also grass, forbs, and accumulated dead
branches and leaves on the forest floor.

In the case of old-growth Araucaria pine, the trunks of the old
trees were large and, under normal circumstances, difficult to ignite.
Unfortunately, however, the most plentiful understory plant in this
region is a species of bamboo called *Quila* (*Chusquea* sp.) and it can be
extremely plentiful wherever some sunlight breaks through the not
overly dense crown system of the pines. Its plentiful and intrusive
woody stems can make walking through the understory very difficult,
and painful, as the broken stems have sharp ends.

Secondly, the fuels must be dry enough to ignite and once
ignited, then remain ignited. *Quila* stems are small, only about a half

115

inch in diameter, and dry stems easily ignite. Thirdly, environmental factors such as relative humidity, moisture content of the fuels, and wind must be favorable for the fire to continue to burn. Lastly, there must be a source of ignition, in other words, something to start the fire. In forests near to population areas, ignition is often in the form of careless human activity such as a discarded cigarette. In more remote areas, fires often are started from what are called dry lightning strikes, in which there is lightning but no associated precipitation to quell the resulting flames. Occasionally fires are started by arsonists.

The spring of 1983 started out dry. The preceding winter had not produced much snow and the spring flora in general was sparse indeed. Many people planted gardens but soon realized that the effort might have been in vain. The *Quila* plants normally flower rather lightly every year but every ten years or so, produce extremely abundant flower crops and then, when the stems die back, this produces much heavier than normal amounts of understory fuels. This happened to be the year when the *Quila* plants had a heavy flower crop, and then the stems died back, producing a much heavier quantity of dry fuels.

By early December 1983, the dreaded *"Sur Negro"* winds (black southerlys) out of the south had begun. These steady winds originate at the South Pole and as they move north, carry extremely dry, cold winds from the south. The winds blow northward along the length of southern Chile, drying the already dry land and the vegetation. *Sur Negro* winds only occur once every decade or so but their arrival usually means a much higher danger of forest fires, and to a lesser extent, agricultural fires.

Unless a parcel of forest land is bordered by a river or agricultural crop land, or a highway, all of which serve as natural fire breaks, forest fires during a *"Sur Negro"* event have the potential to burn intensively during most of the summer until early fall rains reduce moisture content of the fuels. This year was particularly grave as a heavy flower production of the *Quila* plants coincided with the arrival of the *Sur Negro* winds. Maturation, and subsequent death, of the

116

delicate flowers produced a lot of flash fuels making it easy for any possible fire to ignite. Concurrent death of the stems resulted in even more fuels, these heavier and able to sustain and produce a hotter fire and perhaps ignite large Araucaria pine trees. The Araucaria tree is a conifer and produces a large amount of resin in the foliage and in the wood and bark. Once a large tree is ignited, these resins flash evaporate and can create explosive conditions.

Robert and *Rosa* were awakened early one morning by a frantic pounding on the door. As Robert arose and threw on his robe, he noticed that there appeared to be a faint yellow-reddish glow in the south, but when he looked at his watch he noted that it was too early for the sunrise. Before he arrived at the door, he already had formulated a plan of attack for what he knew was going to be a fire of gigantic proportions and a great danger to the village of *Lonquimay*, and their house! As he opened the door he recognized the mayor of *Lonquimay*. *"Buenos días, Don Gustavo. ¡Que placer de verte tan temprano!"* greeted Robert. ("Good morning, *Gustavo*. What a pleasure to see you so early in the morning!")

"Perdoname, Don Roberto, pero hay un problema que veine en nuestra dirección," replied Gustavo. ("Please forgive me the intrusion so early, but there is a problem that is coming in our direction.")

"¿Adelante Gustavo, qué pasa?" asked Robert. ("Come in *Gustavo*, what is happening?") *Rosa* came into the entry room as *Gustavo* and Robert closed the door and entered. *"Ola Gustavo,"* she said with a smile and a wave of her hand. *"Buenos días, señora,"* he replied.

"Roberto y Rosa, perdoname, pero vengo con noticias de algo mal que esta pasando. Uds. recuerdan que los inversionistas de Santiago que pusieron el aserradero unos kilometros al sur de aquí en los terrenos nuestros. El día antes ayer, un grupo de indios demonstraeron cerca del aserradero. Uds. saben como es,- - - cambiaron gritos y insultos, etcetera," explained *Gustavo*. ("Excuse me Robert and *Rosa*, I'm afraid I have some bad news to convey. Do you remember the investors from *Santiago* who put the sawmill on tribal lands several kilometers south of here? The day before yesterday

several tribal members went there and demonstrated against them. You know how it is, - - - words and insults were exchanged.)

"Bueno, a parece que acto de venganza, unos obreros prendían fuego a los terrenos nuestros al lado. Fué una tontera quizás, para asustar el grupo demonstrando. Pero los estupidos del norte no se sabían el peligro de la seqía. El fuego ya esta aumentando y el viento está llevandolo por aquí, a Lonquimay y a su casa," dijo Gustavo. ("In retaliation, several workers at the sawmill started a small fire on adjacent tribal lands and taunted the Indians to put it out. But these stupid northerners didn't realize the danger of what they were doing, and the fire immediately got out of control. The wind is carrying it towards us, here to *Lonquimay*, and to your house I might add.*")*

"¿Por favor, Roberto, Ud. nos puede ayudar, o recomendar lo que se pudría hacer para salvar nuestro pueblo?" quiered *Gustavo.* ("Please, Robert, can you help us, or at least recommend what we might do? We know you have experience with fighting forest fires and we need help to save our town.")

Such a conflagration had never occurred in recent history in the hills surrounding the valley upstream from *Curacautín* to the Argentine border. In most of southern Chile, during normal summer weather in which the *"Sur Negro"* winds were absent, forest or plantation fires were relatively uncommon as a shallow water table allowed active plant growth during the summer. When the occasional fire did occur, the Chilean police force, the *Carabineros*, had a crack forest fire suppression team that had a sterling record of professionalism of quickly suppressing such fires. In most cases of plantation or forest fires in the Central Valley, the *Carabineros* fought these fires mostly with water by digging a shallow pit and placing a suction tube from a portable gasoline powered water pump.

The military government in *Santiago* provided little assistance to combat fires in this region at this time. Ownership of the ancient tribal lands had been in contention during the past century. Some previous governments were sympathetic to their cause but the military government was not and it wanted to end the Indian land ownership problem. It was felt that it would be a good lesson to the *Pehuenches* living in the valley and help convince them to not fight the takeover of their lands by special interests. So, as the fire danger increased, little effort to assist the *Pehuenches* appeared to be forthcoming.

The mountains surrounding *Lonquimay* were covered with dense forests of Araucaria pines. The forest cover continued from the lands bordering the *Naranjo* River Valley and then west across the *Biobío* River valley and as far to the east as the Argentine border. This forest type covered thousands of acres and represented a rich resource for the *Peheunche* people.

From his past experience as a smokejumper, Robert knew that decisive actions needed to be taken and taken now rather than some time later. Robert immediately dressed and set out with *Gustavo* to the mayor's office. *Rosa* would come a little later after *Paulina* was awake and the livestock were taken care of. The first thing Robert did when at the mayor's office was to request a map of the area between the sawmill and *Lonquimay*. He had hiked in that area but needed to be refreshed as to the exact geography. What was available was not a topographic map but rather a simple line drawing with the watercourses drawn in, but better than nothing, thought Robert.

Gustavo penciled in the estimated height of the mountains between each of the watercourses and noted that there were three mountain ranges between the sawmill and the *Naranjo* River. Robert sat down and began to think about possible strategies. He began to feel an increasing sense of dread.

At eight A.M. others began to come into the mayor's office and the mayor explained what they were considering. After a dozen or so were assembled, Robert outlined what he thought should be done, or what could be done with their limited resources. Just after he started, two *Carabineros* also arrived. They were normally stationed in *Curacautín*, but *Lonquimay* was a part of their extended responsibility.

Robert instinctively knew that a ground assault on the fire and the construction of fire-limiting control lines would be too dangerous, especially with the quantity and dryness of the fuels, added to that the continued blowing of the wind. Plus, there were too few potential fire fighters and no equipment except for some farm implements. Robert recalled the famous series of fires in 1910 in Idaho and considered that a series of back-fires might be effective and really was the recourse realistically available to them. During the Idaho fire many individual fires had grown in intensity and combined to form a super conflagration that seemed to have a mind of its own and even jumped across rivers and lakes.

He recalled working in the Tally Lake Ranger District before the year he started smokejumping and remembered marveling how the 1910 Idaho fire had jumped across the several mile-wide Tally Lake. A witness said that the fire arrived at the lake's edge, hesitated a long second, and then simply jumped across the lake. In that second, the heat of the fire had volatilized the pine oils and terpenes and ignited them and then the slope across the lake had simply exploded in flames.

Robert knew that backfires would be the only realistic tool they had that could be effective in this situation, but they also could be dangerous to start and manage. The steep mountains might allow a fire to jump across the intervening valley and ignite the slope on the other side and trap the fighters between the two fires. He recalled the Mann Gulch fire in Montana in 1949 in which 12 smokejumpers had perished when a seemingly innocuous fire had jumped across a ravine below them and then quickly burned upslope to trap them before they could escape.

In order to facilitate an effective control of the fire, Robert and *Gustavo* set up the first command post in the mayor's office in the village of *Lonquimay*. Robert knew from past experience that a quick response was necessary, even though he wasn't sure what that response might end up being. He asked *Gustavo* to appoint a dozen trusted individuals as foremen, individuals he could trust to do what they were

120

told to do. Each foreman was to be in charge of a dozen equally trust-worthy men. These crews would need to move rapidly to wherever they were needed, whether it was to set backfires or put out spot fires that were certain to appear. They had no radios. The *Carabineros* likewise had no radios, only a telephone link to the regional headquarters in *Temuco*.

Gustavo, along with the *Carabineros*, needed to commandeer several pickup trucks and drivers to patrol the highway alongside the *Naranjo* River. Each truck would carry half of a crew. Their job was to simply drive back and forth between pre-established points along the road. When a spot fire occurred, they were to drop off the half-crew to remain and control the spot fire, and go to the staging point to pick up the other half-crew and continue with their patrol. Robert suspected, and hoped, that none of them might ever see a spot fire but someone had to be there in case they did occur.

The biggest communication problem was between the valleys. There were no roads that could support vehicular traffic. So, Robert set up a field command post just across the *Naranjo* River from town. His plan was to send in a small crew to set a series of control burns on the east side of the creek closest to the sawmill. The biggest problem was that of quick communication. The crew had to be able to communicate with him and he had to be able to send messages to them.

As the crew prepared to carry out their mission, Robert told them that they must walk quickly the length of the creek up to its source and then as quickly as they could move back downstream, set fires in a steady line as they walked back. They had no flares or other fire starting equipment so Robert had an idea. Each crew would carry several jugs of kerosene with them. When they were to start the backfires, several men would move along quickly, sloshing a little kerosene onto suitable vegetation and then move along.

Two men following them would also be quickly following them but would only be striking stick matches and throwing the ignited matches onto the kerosene-soaked vegetation. They would not stop to make sure each site ignited, and lose time, they would move quickly along and keep striking and throwing lighted matches. If only a portion of the fires ignited, they would quickly coalesce with nearby fires in the now very flammable kerosene-soaked vegetation. If they were lucky, these fires would coalesce and quickly form one big front as it moved up the hill. Hopefully it would reach the top of the mountain before the fire near the sawmill arrived at the top and then the two would merge and die down for lack of fuels.

Robert wasn't very happy about it but *Rosa* volunteered to ride horseback and relay communications back and forth. She was excellent with horses and was probably the best person available for this job. She would go with this first crew to the base of the stream and wait for them to set the backfires, and then ride back to inform Robert what they had done while the crew walked back to the field command post.

But, as luck would have it, when *Rosa* and the first crew arrived at the base of the creek, they could see that the fire had already topped the hill by the sawmill and was just beginning to move downslope at a fast walk. So, Rosa galloped back to Robert as the crew began their walk back.

Before *Rosa* arrived, Robert had already guessed as to what was happening. He saw a tremendous column of smoke building up as the fire moved up the first mountain slope. Then when the fire arrived at the top of the mountain, it seemed to stop for several long seconds. Then there was a mighty roar, as if a thousand freight trains were rolling past at the same time.

The ground shook, and this was accompanied by a mighty flash of flame, as the fire jumped across the first valley and ignited the vegetation on the opposite mountain-side. This is what had happened during the Idaho fire in 1910. The heat of the fire was so intense that it volatilized the organic materials in the vegetation and then ignited all in one mighty flash and roar. The flash of light and roar elicited shouts and screams in *Lonquimay*. Some people began praying.

122

When Robert saw and realized what was happening, he knew that to attempt a second back fire along the next stream would be too risky, because as fast as the fire had moved, they would have to depend on only one more back fire and that was at the bottom of the hill along the *Naranjo* River. Thank goodness *Rosa* was back and he asked her to ride to all the ground crews along the river and tell them that he was planning to set a series of back fires at the bottom of the mountain next to the river and that they would need to start the fires as soon as *Rosa* rode up with the order. The first backfires should be in back of their house. He would be there to extinguish any spot fires that developed near their house or outbuildings. *Gustavo* would remain with him to relay any last minute instructions to the other fire fighters.

The fire fighters would then need to be especially vigilant to seek and quickly suppress spot fires that would certainly start from such a close series of backfires. During the next few minutes, *Rosa* played a vital role as she galloped back and forth on horseback relaying commands to the fire fighters and their responses to Robert who was now on the line, issuing commands as the need arose.

The spot fires coalesced quickly and the collective backfire swept up the slope. The combined backfires actually created a strong wind that roared up the slope. Embers flew into the air and were blown back toward town by higher winds. Some embers landed in town and started small fires that were suppressed by the town's fire department crew and residents. Everyone worked through the night as the fire eventually died down due to the slight moisture uptake by the fuels as the relative humidity rose. When daylight returned, the steadily increasing glow from the other side indicated that their backfire might prove to have worked. By noon the other fire arrived at the top of the mountain and spit angry showers of embers onto the town of *Lonquimay.* By now, though, not much could scare these people as they worked wearily to extinguish the last of the small spot fires scattered here and there.

They had done it! With cooperation of virtually all the adults in the town, and with their faith in Robert's wildfire fighting experience, a miracle had been performed! Just before noon on that day, several busloads of *Carabinero* fire fighters arrived in town to patrol the burned over areas and extinguish small fires. Thousands of acres of prime Araucaria pine forest had been lost, but the *"Sur Negro"* had done its worst and the town of *Lonquimay* had survived! And the rest of the Araucaria pine forest north of the river had survived! And, their house had survived!

Early the next morning, as townspeople assembled in the town plaza to greet the dozens of fire fighters coming in, Robert met *Rosa* and said, "Well, honey, we did it, you did it!" They embraced and hugged for a long time, just standing there in each other's arms. As they just stood there, hugging each other, they became aware of people standing around them.   As they parted, dozens of people came up, shook their hands and said, *"Gracias Roberto y Rosa por un trabajo bien hecho."* ("Thank you Robert and *Rosa* for a job well done.") After awhile Robert and *Rosa* looked at each other and Robert said, "Come on. Lets go home. Our beautiful house is filled with smoke but at least it is still standing and not just a pile of ashes."

As they walked home Robert suddenly recalled that moment a decade earlier when *Rosa* had given herself to him and that the fire today had incinerated that area as well as the *canelo* grove with it's unique single *misodendrum* infestation.

Quila – (redrawn from *Muñoz*, 1959)

Chapter 19
A Last Challenge
1983

In January of the previous year, two plant pathologists from the Department of Plant Pathology at the University of Minnesota had returned from a plant-collecting trip in southern Chile. They had gone to Chile on a foray specifically to collect forest pathology specimens. One of the pathologists was a specialist in parasitic plants and he had collected quite a number of pressed and whole specimens of various species of *misodendrum*. The pressed specimens were packed in a bundle and some not pressed larger specimens were packaged in cardboard boxes.

Although they had a USDA certificate to collect these specimens, when they returned to the United States at the Miami airport, the overly zealous USDA inspector there insisted on sending the specimens to their Washington, D. C. facility for further inspection and fumigation. While the specimens were enroute back from Washington, the truck carrying them crashed and one of the boxes was ripped apart. Most, but not all, of the specimens were eventually recovered and forwarded to the scientists at the University in St. Paul.

A week or so after the excitement of the fire in *Lonquimay* dissipated and there was a return to normalcy, *Rosa* began to complain of occasional pains in her abdomen. They had begun several days after the fire had been brought under control. She thought that perhaps the nearly constant bouncing up and down on a galloping horse had stretched or broken something lose in her abdomen, causing the pain.

But, the pains persisted. After several weeks had passed and the pains got worse, Robert insisted that she have a medical examination. A visit to the doctor in *Temuco* quickly resulted in another visit, this time in *Santiago*. The specialist there said she thought that

Rosa had stage-2 ovarian cancer and that it needed to be removed immediately.

Ovarian cancer is a terrible disease for an individual to experience. The cancer starts when cells in the ovary begin to grow out of control. In healthy ovaries, normal cells replace cells that wear out and die or to repair injuries. However, sometimes abnormal cancerous cells are formed and, instead of dying, continue to grow and divide and create new abnormal cells to soon form a tumor. These cells can eventually move into the bloodstream or lymph vessels of the body.

Many types of tumors can start in the ovaries. Some tumors are benign and these can be surgically removed by removing that ovary or the part of the ovary containing the tumor. Other tumors are malignant or cancerous. In these cases, the treatment options become much more involved, complex, and sometimes much more problematic.

The three main treatment options include: surgery, chemotherapy, and radiation therapy. Surgery is the most common treatment to simply remove the cancerous cells. But, chemotherapy uses chemical medications that travel through the bloodstream to destroy cancerous cells growing both inside and outside the ovaries. Radiation treatment, using high-energy X-rays to kill cancer cells, was seldom used at that time.

Robert and *Rosa* discussed the diagnosis and, after little hesitancy, decided to go to the United States for another diagnosis. Robert made arrangements for them to fly that week to see another specialist, this time in the Mayo Clinic in Rochester, Minnesota.

Robert had placed most of his plant-collecting income, and his military pay while in the hospital, in savings and they could easily afford the trip, and although they had no health insurance, decided to go regardless of the expense. The visit to Mayo confirmed what the doctor in *Santiago* had told them, but now the tumor had advanced to a stage 4, and the several specialists with whom they had consulted did not now recommend surgical removal of the tumor. It was too late!

126

Rosa was feeling so much pain now that she was afraid to fly and so she and Robert decided to go to his parents' home in Missoula. She was afraid that she would die here rather than in Chile, but at least she would be with Robert and *Paulina*, and Robert's wonderful parents.

As *Rosa* and Robert left the hospital they continued to discuss their options, which they realized were virtually non-existent. Normally, if detected early enough, ovarian cancer was removed by surgery and then the patient was given a serious of radiation treatments and perhaps chemical therapy. But, in *Rosa's* case, the cancer had progressed too rapidly! The prognosis was not good and all that could be done was for *Rosa* to be kept as comfortable as possible.

Robert and *Rosa* were in shock and *Rosa* and *Paulina* were in tears, but they began to discuss what they might do. Their discussion continued as they entered the parking lot to their rental car and, as they arrived at the car, a small sagebrush-like growth of plant material blew against *Rosa's* leg, startling her. Robert glanced at it and instantly recognized it as being a witches' broom of *misodendrum*. He remarked, "How strange that it should be here in Minnesota."

Rosa, though, gasped and grabbed Robert's hand! She had instantly suspected that it was some kind of message from her mother! She then recalled conversations with her grandmother *Luisa* several months before she died, when Robert was still in the coma. *Luisa* had told her that the *misodendrum* plant had some powerful attributes but it was extremely dangerous to use without great care.

Luisa told her that a *misodendrum* plant infecting a sacred *canelo* tree was especially powerful. Unfortunately, historically this combination had such powerful attributes that, although once fairly common in southern Chile, it had been collected so heavily that *canelo* trees infected with *misodendrum* were basically extinct. It had an almost prehistoric history of medicinal powers that none of the modern-day *Pehuenches* now understood. That knowledge had been lost! And the only relict-infected *canelo* had been incinerated in the forest fire earlier that year. Robert kicked himself for not having done anything more

127

about it before the fire. They both recalled the letter that *Claudia* had left for *Rosa* and discussed what it might mean. Robert had an idea!

Most medicinal plants gained their efficacy from certain extractives such as essential oils, alkaloids, and other metabolic by-products. In fact, success of the entire medicinal plant industry was based on this premise. Previously, scientists at Pharmtec had extracted some essential oils and other metabolic components from *misodendrum* plants. They were actually quite rich in certain essential oils. But, Robert's boss had told him that the *misodendrum* leaves from the *canelo* infection was especially rich in a variety of essential oils and other components that they had not identified because of the small amount of tissue that Robert had sent.

Robert wondered if some of these components could help *Rosa*. Were there any *canelo* extracts left? His boss said, "Yes, they had been freeze-dried but the amount was very small." The problem was that even if they had a larger amount, they did not know which portions might be efficacious. Robert did not know if they should be injected, taken orally, or what. At the worst, *Rosa* could perhaps be poisoned if he guessed wrong. At best, she would likely die of the cancer.

As they discussed the dangers, *Rosa's* response was that she was going to die a horrible death anyway and she wanted to take a chance with whatever strategy Robert could devise. Robert conjectured that they should use the extract in as natural a state as possible. Ancestors of the natives had apparently used the *misodendrum/canelo* combination in the distant past and they did not have fancy equipment with which to make sophisticated extracts, so Robert felt that a ground-up concoction of plant material steeped in hot water was likely to be their best chance. And, since the ancients did not have sophisticated injection equipment either, the best chance seemed to be that *Rosa* should either drink the steeped liquid or rub it into the skin on her abdomen. They did both with the tiny amount of available material.

128

Robert performed the treatments once because there was only enough material for one treatment. He had no idea if it would work or not and he had used up valuable time. Two months had passed since *Rosa* first noticed the pains. And she seemed to be noticeably failing each day. Would the treatment work? *Rosa* would lose her life if it didn't and there was not even the slightest hint that it might work.

Finally, *Rosa's* health failed to the point where she could no longer ingest food, or even drink the very small amount of steeped liquid remaining of *misodendrum/canelo* concoction. She grew weaker and weaker and finally went into a coma. They made her as comfortable as they could and waited for the end. Robert and *Paulina* were with her constantly. Robert sensed that the spirit of *Claudia* was there as well although he saw no vision of her.

Misodendrum brachystachium – (redrawn from *Muñoz*, 1959)

Chapter 20
The New Cemetery, *Lonquimay* Valley
1990

It was a day of festivity! Robert and *Paulina* loaded the car at the house and departed for the new cemetery. At this time, *Paulina* was now a beautiful 17-yr-old young lady and Robert was very proud of her. They followed a few other cars up the mountain road as first dozens and, then hundreds, of other *Pehuenche* tribe members joined the caravan. Robert parked the car at the foot of the mountain where the new cemetery was to be located.

Shortly after the coup in 1973, false claimants had appealed to the sympathetic military dictatorship to claim that the *Pehuenche* ownership of much of the tribal land was false and obtained the legal right to do whatever they wished with the land. This included harvesting the Araucaria pine forests that were prevalent there. Tribal elders had lost title to the land where the old cemetery was located and, and after continued desecrations by military sympathizers, decided to relocate it to a more secure site, deep in now-secure tribal lands.

Robert unlocked the trunk and removed the funerary box containing the bones of *Claudia* while *Paulina* removed the box containing the bones of her grandfather *Juan*. Even though she was only a baby when he was killed, she felt a great affection for him, as she did for her grandmother *Claudia*. She wished that they had the remains of her uncle *Miguel* but nobody knew where he was buried, if in fact he ever had been buried. At any rate, today they would erect a **goji totum** in his memory so his spirit would have a place to rest at this now holy of places.

Robert had been raised as a Catholic, but he had seen enough mysteries since he had come to Chile and lived among the *Pehuenches* that he had a healthy respect for their religion. At the new site, they placed the boxes on the ground and turned to retrieve another set. Their hearts, and especially Robert's, were heavy as he remembered *Claudia* and *Juan* and how they had come to such untimely, and needless, deaths.

As Robert and *Paulina* paced back down the trail, Robert's thoughts shifted to reflect on the incredibly satisfying life he had experienced so far here in Chile. It was all due to *Rosa* and her wonderful family. Now he had his and *Rosa's* daughter, *Paulina*, and the love and respect of the residents of *Lonquimay*. As *Rosa* and her entourage approached in another car, through tears he could see that many other cars had arrived and people were unloading more funerary boxes of relatives. Others were unloading packages of picnic materials and laying out picnic blankets.

He said to *Paulina*, "Honey, do you remember that day 10 years ago when we thought we were losing your mother? How exhausted we all were after sitting by her bedside for almost 2 weeks. And then I went to the extra bedroom and fell asleep. As in a dream I thought I heard someone speaking in Spanish and then as I awoke realized that it was your grandmother *Claudia* speaking with your mother. You heard them as well and ran into my room shouting, *"Papá, Papá,* come, come, *Mamá* is better and is sitting up in bed," and how we both ran in and there she was, alive! Do you remember, *Paulina*, of the joy we felt?" *Paulina* answered with an expression of joy on her face, "Yes, *Papá*, I remember!"

Almost every one of the *Pehuenches* living in the valley appeared to be at the site of the new cemetery today and all were dressed in their finest traditional costumes. Most were laughing, some were singing, children were running from side to side, screaming of happiness and joy. How lucky he felt to be a part of this remarkable group of people. Then, his eyes misted over as he saw *Rosa* stepping out of the car, dressed in the shining silver-trimmed regalia of a tribal **machi**. She smiled when he gave a little wave and she waved back.

Robert was so grateful that *Rosa's* grandmother had known about a possible remedy to use in attacking the ovarian tumor. The remedy apparently proved to be very effective but the secret of its effectiveness was the essential oil in the lipid material from the *misodendrum/canelo* combination that the lab at Pharmtec had extracted, purified, and concentrated. One of the most serious obstacles in the cancer treatment had been how to get the chemical into the tumor. And, no one in 1990 yet knew how it worked!

Canelo - **FOYE** (redrawn from *Muñoz*, 1959)

Chapter 21
New Orleans, Louisiana
2000
Annual Meeting of the American Phytopathological Society

A year later, in 1991, *Paulina*, along with her parents, decided that she would study for her Bachelor's degree in the United States. She was now 18 years old. She was accepted at the now University of Montana, from where Robert had graduated several decades earlier when it was then known as Montana State University. She, like her father, also studied botany. Her intention at that time was to learn as much as she could about medicinal plants and then study for a Master's degree in chemistry.

By the time *Paulina* began her studies, the general physiology of plants was pretty well understood and a great shift in research was underway to understand the ecology of plant/environment interactions. She did well at the university. By 1999, when she was 26 years old and married, she and her husband, another doctoral student, Nanno Mulder from Holland whom she met during her graduate studies, were finishing their doctorates at the University of Minnesota. For her doctorate she had enrolled in the Department of Genetics and Cell Biology and he had enrolled in the Department of Plant Pathology. They made a complimentary, and eventually formidable, team.

During the time of her graduate studies, *Paulina's* life took an unexpected turn. The field of molecular genetics was exploding. Gene sequencing was becoming very popular, and useful in many different areas of biology. So, when *Paulina* took a special problems course to learn the technique of gene sequencing and needed a project, she decided to focus on some aspect of medicinal plants, but with an unusual twist. All her life she had been committed to learning as much as she could about her *Pehuenche* ancestors and their close relationship with medicinal plants. So, for this problem, which then soon led to the

133

main theme of her doctoral dissertation, she chose to do genetic sequencing of the native Araucanian Indians in southern Chile.

As she started her sequencing research, she did the first trials with her own blood. To her surprise, much of her DNA had areas with high rates of methylation. She did not know what this might mean. An important finding when she explored this aspect further was that virtually all of the *Pehuenches* whose blood that she had sampled and sequenced also had an unusually high percentage of methylated DNA. At that time no one knew what had caused the high rates of methylation of DNA, or what it might mean.

As she became drawn into the excitement of this work, she wondered if her mother's DNA also had a high rate of methylation. So, she asked her mother to send a mouth swab from which she could obtain a genetic sequence. Surprisingly, her mother had a relatively low percentage of methylated DNA. The next time she called her parents in Chile she mentioned this to her father. He recalled that his business partners in Hamilton, Montana probably still had blood samples of *Rosa* from before she had been diagnosed and treated for ovarian cancer. *Paulina* got those samples and ran another series of sequencing and methylation tests. DNA from those samples was heavily methylated!

She gave a seminar on her research to the department and afterward a colleague in another department mentioned that in her laboratory they had identified one of the DNA sequences that initiated the immune response in humans. When they tested and compared *Rosa's* early and later DNA samples, their work revealed that the major gene regulating the immune response was methylated in the early blood samples and not methylated in the later samples.

What did all this mean? Her frantic research activity, and then that of her husband, came to a sudden focus when fellow scientists on the planning board of the American Phytopathological Society suggested that the two of them were to be selected as keynote speakers at the proposed "Symposium on the Interaction of Plant Pathogens on the Success of Medicinal Plants" at the next annual meeting which was to be held in New Orleans, Louisiana.

Each year the planning committee faced the rather daunting task of identifying a new or emerging area of research focus that was so new that it had not acquired much national attention but with enough solid research to indicate that it represented a new and innovative research thrust, something that might be of value to prospective attendees and useful for their research planning. The use of medicinal plants was becoming very popular at this time and one focus of this presentation, to be presented by Nanno Mulder, was to summarize some of the major plant pathogenic diseases of these medicinal plants.

Plant pathologists, and especially extension specialists, had to be familiar with these new diseases if they were to be useful to a concerned public. And, research planners had to know what diseases were increasing in incidence or importance so they could plan useful research for their control. The second focus of the symposium, to be presented by *Paulina*, was not as well understood by the planning committee, but her graduate advisor assured the committee that her presentation would be provocative.

So, exactly one year later, in a crowded auditorium of several hundred eager plant pathology students, technicians, professors, and members of the press, *Paulina* and Nanno sat at the left end of the front row waiting to be introduced. *Paulina* sat between her parents, *Rosa* and Robert, and her two children, *Sebastian* and *Alexandra*.

Nanno introduced his talk by presenting several slides showing lists, and some drawings and photographs, of medicinal plants, not only those known in Chile, but from around the world. After a brief description of the plants and the remedies they were responsible for, he opened the main theme of his presentation by remarking, "The amazing fact about most of these medicinal plants is that they have very few diseases! Why is this?"

His next slide showed a summary of all known medicinal plants in Europe, Asia, North America, and South America to summarize the major point of his presentation. In this slide was a graph showing two more or less horizontal lines, but one ascending and one descending. He said, "The ascending linear regression line represents all the medicinal plants from around the world that have been studied in many laboratories and that are known to synthesize various secondary metabolites that have known positive medicinal effects on humans. The declining regression line represents the known number of diseases affecting each particular plant, regardless as to whether they are caused by fungi, bacteria, viruses, or mycoplasmas. Notice the sharp decline in that line toward the right side of the graph. So, what this graph is saying is that the more secondary metabolites a plant has, the fewer diseases it also has. It is a statistically significant relationship."

He continued, "I will briefly explain why that is. To begin, we must have an understanding of the important metabolic pathways present in plants. A simplified outline of primary and secondary metabolism is shown in this diagram:"

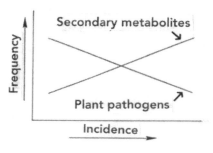

This graph depicts the relationship between the frequency of secondary metabolites and the incidence of plant diseases in green plants.

As he continued his presentation, he pointed his laser light at the various parts of the diagram as he described each of them. "The major physiologic pathway in green plants is that of photosynthesis. Photosynthesis utilizes the sun's energy to make glucose, which is the energy-containing carbon skeleton starting point for all of the subsequent major metabolic pathways in plants. Glucose is quickly produced and stored as starch until needed and then is

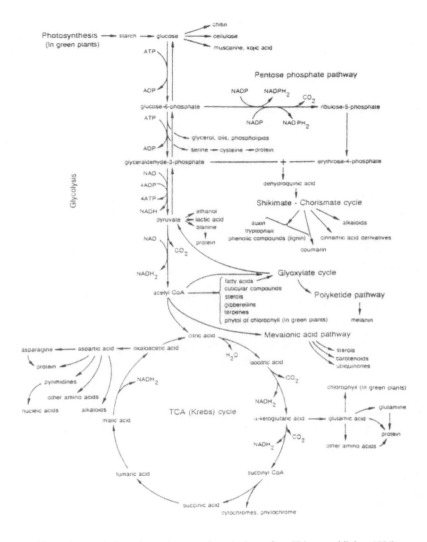

The major metabolic pathways in green plants (redrawn from Tainter and Baker, 1996)

137

eventually transformed, as needed, into cell walls and many other carbon-containing components."

"Plants are able to use this energy via a process called metabolism. There are two major forms of metabolism, primary and secondary, that are active in green plants. Primary metabolism is responsible for the degradation of organic molecules, such as glucose, and for the production of energy and synthesis of lipids, carbohydrates, nucleic acids, and proteins. So, primary metabolism involves two basic aspects that are opposite in their actions but complimentary in their effects."

"The pathways of secondary metabolism usually are only synthetic and produce metabolites that have no obvious cellular function but do tend to be specific for a particular group of plants." Nanno then made a general circular gesture toward the drawing on the screen and continued.

"Pathways of secondary metabolism are particularly important for students seeking possible medicinal properties. Secondary metabolism is usually more prevalent after the active growth resulting from primary metabolism has ceased. Many secondary metabolites have no known physiologic function to the plant that produces them. They are usually produced through the Mevalonic acid pathway, the Polyketide pathway, or the Shikimate pathway."

He continued and pointed at each of these pathways on the diagram as he spoke, "The production of secondary metabolites may be a way in which plants remove and compartmentalize excess intermediates before they become toxic to that plant. They may coincidently serve the function of preventing invasion by pathogenic fungi or insects and their production has the major secondary benefit of allowing them to survive in a dog-eat-dog world."

"A well-known example of toxic secondary metabolites is the large amount of polyphenolics produced by the Shikimate-Chorismate cycle following wounding of plant tissues. These metabolites are toxic to many potentially invading fungal pathogens, and even insects, and prevent subsequent infection or infestation. The brown color of a partially eaten apple, and some other fruits, is due to the oxidation of these phenolic materials and is a naturally evolved plant defense mechanism. So, now we can speculate as to why medicinal plants have few pathogenic diseases."

"In essence, medicinal plants have high concentrations of certain toxic metabolic byproducts, which for humans coincidently may have some medicinal properties, but for plants, these toxic materials help to protect them from infection by disease-causing organisms, or even infestation by insects. A good example for us today is the Chilean shrub, *boldo*. If one had to choose the most famous Chilean medicinal plant it would probably be this one. *Boldo* contains the alkaloid boldine and the chemical ascaridole that gives *boldo* its assertive flavor. Ascaridole is highly toxic and produces abortfacient and teratogenic effects in rats and has abortive qualities if used during pregnancy in people. In certain people it may be toxic in large amounts and has antifungal, antibacterial, and antiviral qualities."

Nanno closed his presentation with this summary: "I happen to be familiar with many medicinal plants native to Chile, the country of birth of my beautiful wife who is sitting in the front row and who will continue this presentation. Her father worked as a medicinal plant explorer in Chile and his business partners studied many of the Chilean medicinal plants. Their hypothesis, which led to the formation of a successful business, was that medicinal plant remedies in Chile had undergone thousands of years of practical experimentation by native peoples to determine their effectiveness."

"Their company collected many of these plants and extracted major secondary metabolites, and then began to correlate the different extractives with whatever sickness or disease the native peoples had employed them for. With the Chilean medicinal plant remedies they knew that they had a long tradition of effectiveness and it was just a matter of identifying those plants that were the most effective."

He introduced his conclusion with a list which he pointed to as he spoke, "Some of the secondary metabolites tested in their laboratory included: alkaloids, cinnamic acid derivatives, coumarin, and phenolic compounds from the Shikimate-Chorismate cycle; melanin from the Polyketide pathway; sterols, carotinoids; and ubiquinones from the Mevalonic acid pathway. All of the plant pathologists here already know that many of these compounds are toxic to plant pathogens. My current research is focused on exactly how these metabolites operate as medicinal remedies."

Nanno finished his presentation by introducing his wife, "My wife, *Paulina*, has worked on an off-shoot of this work and will share with us her interesting findings in the next presentation. I think you will see that serendipity is real and sometimes you can't predict where your research will lead you, even with best of planning."

After the applause for Nanno had died down, *Paulina* came to the podium and spread out her notes. "Hi, my name is *Paulina* Mulder. My presentation will begin by sharing with you a little of my family history. In 1983 my mother was diagnosed with ovarian cancer. In the few weeks between the initial diagnosis and her arrival at the Mayo Clinic in Minnesota the cancer had progressed from a stage 2 to a stage 4. The future did not look good for my mother. The specialists at Mayo said that there was no hope and that surgery or other treatment would be futile. My mother prepared to die. But, my father did not lose hope. He had learned many years earlier, as a forest fire fighter, that when you are fighting a really big fire, any action is better than doing nothing."

"When he was collecting medicinal plants years earlier in Chile he was extremely interested in a parasitic plant that was, and still is, fairly common on many species of *Nothofagus* in the southern part of Chile. My grandmother had told my mother of some mysterious powers of that parasitic plant when it was parasitizing another Chilean tree called *canelo*. *Canelo* is a medicinal plant and was considered sacred by the native peoples. Many native people had also known about its

140

strange and unusual powers and over the years had, unfortunately, harvested virtually all *canelo* trees infected with the *misodendrum* parasite, so much so that infected *canelo* became virtually extinct."

"My grandmother knew of only a single small grove of *canelo* trees infected with the *misodendrum* parasite. That grove was on her family's property in the mountains south of the village of *Lonquimay*. During my father's last week in Chile, in 1973, just before he was to go to Vietnam as a soldier, she instructed my mother to take him to a small grove of *canelo* trees that had only a few *canelo* trees with a few *misodendrum* parasites growing on their branches. It was the only remaining such grove that she was aware of. My father collected several small samples that he placed in his plant press to dry and then brought these back to the States. As we now know, that sacred grove was a magical place."

She continued with a smile, "For me it was especially magical, because my parents tell me that I was conceived on that very day in that very grove of *canelo* trees." Robert and *Rosa's* faces turned red and they smiled at each other. The audience loved her remark, though, and gave *Paulina* a standing round of applause. She said, "Unfortunately, a decade later that grove, with those few infected *canelo* trees, was completely destroyed by a forest fire."

Then she returned to her presentation, "But, to digress, after my mother was diagnosed with ovarian cancer, and all hope was lost for her recovery, we desperately pondered what we thought was a message left by my grandmother before she was murdered by the military regime. In that message she implied that only my father had the knowledge to save my mother. So, my father administered to mother a ground-up bit of dry *misodendrum* tissue from the *canelo* tree, all that was left of his original samples. But, we were dismayed! There was initially no change in my mother's condition and we prepared for her to die. Then, after about a week's time, she slowly improved and within several weeks she had recovered! Subsequent examinations have shown her to be free of ovarian cancer."

"Surely now, everyone here is thinking, we are scientists and know that this event was probably only chance and there was no real cause and effect supported with credible scientific experimentation. But there persisted in our minds the intriguing possibility that something in the *misodendrum* extract had helped her body fight off the cancer."

She continued, "So, this is my story. We had no idea what might have been in the *misodendrum* extract that saved my mother. But, nearly 20 years after my father had originally sent the *misodendrum* sample to Pharmtec, the company that had employed him to collect medicinal plant samples, he received a package of recent scientific articles from his friends at Pharmtec that began to unravel the puzzle of what might have happened. He immediately called me at the university and relayed what the articles contained."

"With help from my advisor, I restructured my research to take advantage of this new information. Since the discovery in 1953 by Watson and Crick of the double-helix nature of DNA, scientists had produced thousands of research experiments and reams of scientific articles on every imaginable trait and characteristic of DNA and RNA. One of the interesting things discovered at Pharmtec was that extracts of *misodendrum* had a strong ability to demethylate DNA. At the time of that discovery, no one knew what benefit this might provide for the DNA, or for anything else for that matter, and so it was forgotten. What did this fact mean, if anything?"

"When mother was diagnosed with ovarian cancer, father sent samples of her blood to his friends at Pharmtec. They had not known what to do with them so they were placed in storage. After the methylation process of DNA was discovered, Pharmtec scientists, working with me in my early graduate studies, inspected those blood samples and were quite surprised and puzzled to discover that in mother's early blood samples, much DNA was methylated. Several years later, other scientists discovered the significant fact that methylation of the gene controlling the immune response could, in fact, stop activity of the immune system."

She continued, "Now I must give you a brief review of how the body fights infections. In many ways, cancer is an infection by a foreign organism. The first lines of defense against foreign invaders are the white blood cells. Certain specialized white blood cells, called macrophages, destroy any foreign proteins or germs encountered in the body. During an immune response, white blood cells called T cells produce a protein known as interleukin-2 (IL-2). High production of IL-2 sends T cells into overdrive to recognize and attack cancer cells. T cells are killers that use receptors to recognize and then attach these receptors to surface structures called antigens found on the invading protein. However, if the gene that programs production of T cells is kept from being activated, then no T cells, hence, no resistant response is possible."

"What my research revealed was that mother's strange recovery from ovarian cancer was suggested by a series of experimental observations I subsequently made. These early works were extremely crude then because it wasn't until nearly a decade later that gene technology had advanced far enough to prove my hypothesis, just as the roles of individual genes were beginning to be determined. I postulated that perhaps mother's DNA that encoded for the production of IL-2 was methylated and could not recognize the invading cancer protein."

"I did not figure this out from the blue. When I was a graduate student I experimented with my own blood and tried every new analytic technique as it became available. My IL-2 gene was methylated and this methylation was certainly inherited from my mother. Treatment with the essential oil from *misodendrum* removed this methylation from mother's DNA and allowed the affected gene to signal active production of IL-2, thus saving her from certain death from ovarian cancer."

"And, more had been learned of how cancer behaves in the human body. In theory at least, cancer had been thought to act as a foreign body that has invaded the body. The human immune system will normally attack and destroy any such foreign bodies, including tumors. The T-cells can discriminate between foreign and host molecules. They act much like military police to watch over the immune system's defense (and act as soldier cells) to make sure they would kill only foreign invaders and not damage the body's own healthy cells."

"Some cancers can actively interfere with the immune response, and in recent years, have been the object of considerable research effort. That work is not the object of this treatise. There was another reaction, however, which has come to be recognized as perhaps being very important in some instances with certain people."

"In mother's case, methylation of the DNA had stopped activity of the immune system. Something in the dried *misodendrum* extracts had removed the CH_3, or methyl, groups from some of the DNA that was responsible for initiating the immune response in her body. Ovarian cancers, as well as many other cancers, are able to suppress the body's immune system that then allows the cancer to grow unchecked. Methylation of the gene controlling the immune response is one major reason for this suppression."

"A key question is 'what causes this methylation?'" "Soon-to-be-published scientific research reveals that methylation is often caused by exposure to chemical pollutants, or severe trauma. In mother's body, many DNA sites were methylated, and this was probably not a result of the spreading ovarian cancer, but rather the result of some previous significant DNA methylation-causing event, either in her body or in the bodies of one or more of her ancestors. As early as the 1970s it was noted that in many people, many DNA genes had a methyl group on the end of the gene, which effectively prevented expression of that gene. No one then knew why, but it is now known now that, incredibly, these methylated areas can survive several, or even many,

144

generations. In other words, methylated DNA may survive gene desegregation, generation, and translocation to a new individual!"

"In mother's case, something in past generations may have caused this methylation. Perhaps it resulted from the trauma suffered by her grandfather Jean during World War I. Maybe it resulted in her maternal ancestors during the great extermination of *Pehuenches* in Argentina during the late 1800s. Or perhaps the trauma was even earlier, when a distant ancestor was seriously injured by a saber-toothed tiger or bear after the crossing of the Beiringian land bridge."

"Maybe the mother of the Anzick boy was so grief stricken that her DNA was methylated, or maybe the sister or mother of Mai'a was so traumatized by her disappearance that their DNA was methylated as a result."

"In closing, though, I am inclined to believe that it was the trauma mother suffered when she returned to the house on that terrible day in 1973 and saw her mother and father lying dead in pools of blood, and perhaps some additional trauma until she knew that I, her baby, was safe."

"To this day we do not know what was in the extract that caused DNA demethylation in my mother, and conicidently saved her life. We have tried many extracts of *misodendrum*, and many from *canelo*, but to no avail. There must have been something in the extract of that particular *misodendrum* plant parasitizing that particular *canelo* tree. Some super-purified essential oil, perhaps, that had the ability to demethylate DNA. We just don't know yet. My father has spent quite some time searching for another natural infection of *misodendrum* on *canelo*, but has found none, yet. He has also tried to artificially inoculate *canelo* trees with *misodendrum*, but so far with no lasting success. The *misodendrum* rootlets are initially able to invade the *canelo* tissue but are soon walled off by wound periderm tissue and the infection dies. You can bet, though, that we have not given up on this quest."

As *Paulina* finished her presentation and answered the last question, another round of applause went forth. Her presentation

145

being over, *Paulina* shuffled and stacked her notes and placed them in her briefcase. The microphone was still on. As the applause began to die down, she paused, and then turned toward her left side of the room, waved, and said, *"Gracias abuelita."*

Rosa and Robert heard what she said – they were stunned! What did that mean? *Rosa* gasped and with one hand covered her mouth and with the other grabbed Robert's arm! Robert looked at her as she pointed to the side of the stage toward where *Paulina* had spoken. There were two visible figures standing there! He recognized the male figure as *Juan*! The female figure was resplendent in silver and *lapis lazuli* jewelry and the costume of a *Pehuenche* **machi**. It was a youthful *Claudia*! She and an equally youthful *Juan* were smiling. And, as they faded from view, both gave a little wave as *Claudia* said, *"Bien hecho, mi nieta"* (Well done, my granddaughter.)

Suggested additional reading

http://en.wikipedia.org/wiki/Boldo

http://www.victorianweb.org/science/darwin/massacre.html

http://en.wikipedia.org/wiki/Conquest_of_the_Desert

Anonymous. Undated. Manual de Plantas Medicinales en La Medicina Casera. Sociedad de Campesino Mapuche. 104 pp.

Anonymous. 2008. Nuevo Manual de Medicina Natural. Ediciones FELC. Araucania 1773. Santiago, Chile. 154 pp.

Anonymous. 2013. Diccionario Mapuche. Editorial Centro Grafico Limitada, Colón 916, La Serena, Chile. 251 pp.

Bower, B. 2014. Bones offer insight into Clovis origins. p. 7, in Science News Magazine. Society for Science and the Public. 1719 N Street, NW, Washington, DC 20036.

Gaidos, S. 2014. T-Force. Science News Magazine. June 14: 22-25.

Garcia, M. A., S. Duk, G. Weigert, M. Silva, and M. Alarcon. 1993. Chromosome aberrations induced by Eumaitenine, a sesquiterpene isolated from *Maytenus boaria* Mol. in cultured CHO cells. Bull. Environ. Contam. Toxicol. 51: 803-897.

Grimm, D. 2015. Dawn of the dog. Science. 348 (Issue 6232): 274-279.

Hodges, G. 2015. The first American. National Geographic. 227 (1): 124-137.

Kornbluh, P. 2003. The Pinochet File – A Declassified Dossier on Atrocity and Accountability. The New Press, New York, London. 551 pp.

Ledford, H. 2014. The killer within. Nature. 508: 23 – 26.

Maclean, N. 1992. Young Men and Fire. University of Chicago Press. 301 pp.

Marean, C. W. 2015. The most invasive species of all. Sci. Amer. 313 (No. 2): 32-39.

Pizarro, Carlos Muñoz. 1966. Sinopsis de la Flora Chilena. Ediciones de la Universidad de Chile, Santiago, Chile. 500 pp.

Raff, J. A. and D. A. Bolnick. 2014. Genetic roots of the first Americans. Nature. 506: 162-163.

Rebolledo, R., J. Abarzua, A. Zavala, A. Quiroz, M. Alvear, and A. Aquilera. 2012. Cienc. Inv, Agr. 39(3): 481-488.

Meiselas, S. (ed.) 1990. Chile From Within - 1973-1988. W.W. Norton & Company, New York and London. 58 pp.

Ruhlen, M. 1987. A Guide to the World's Languages. Volume 1: Classification. Stanford University Press, Stanford, California. 433 pp.

Skinner, M. K, 2014. A new kind of inheritance. Scientific American. 311 (2): 45-51.

Sloan, R. E. 2005. Minnesota Fossils and Fossiliferous Rocks. Published privately in an edition of 1000. 218 pp.

Tainter, F. H. and F. A. Baker. 1996. Principles of Forest Pathology. John Wiley and Sons, Inc., New York. 805 pp.

Urzua, A, R. Santander, J. Echeverria, C. Villalobos, S. M. Palacios, and Y. Rossi. 2010. Insecticidal properties of *Peumus boldus* Mol. essential oil on the house fly, Musca domestica L. Boletin

Latinoamericano y del Caribe de Plantas Medicinales y Aromaticas. 9 (6): 465-469.

Weise, G. A. 2013. Historia de Curacautín – "Testigo de mi Tiempo". Tomo Uno. Imprenta Wesaldi, Temuco, Chile. 418 pp.

Zin, J. S. and C. Weiss R. sin fecha. La Salud por Medio de las Plantas Medicinales. Editorial Don Bosco S. A., Santiago, Chile. 407 pp.

Postscript –

Discovery of what became known as the Anzick child led to an important career choice several years later by one of the family members on whose land the remains were discovered. In 1968, when the remains were discovered, a young Sarah Anzick was only 2 years old. After their discovery, the remains were stored by archeologists for 30 years and then returned to the family in 1968.

At that time, Sarah was working as an undergraduate student on the Human Genome Project, later specializing in cancer genetics. She realized that an examination of the child's bones might reveal important genetic secrets. The team she worked with reconstructed the child's entire genome, indeed, revealing that the Anzick child's family were ancestors of eighty percent of all Native Americans alive today. This finding finally settled the question as to where the first Americans originated.

On a rainy day in June 2014, a group of people including scientists and representatives of North American tribes gathered for a reburial ceremony as Sarah Anzick returned the remains to the control of tribal leaders. Not only were the child's bones among the most important discovered in the Americas, they were reinterred in the place where his people had originally placed them.

Chapter 7 – Medicinal Plants

Robert's fast-growing list of native Chilean medicinal plants and some major remedies included the following. This is not a definitive list, there are many more, depending on local sources:

Ajo – AKU - (*Allium sativum*) – The bulbs are eaten, for flu and fever.

Alcachofa - (*Cynara scolymus*) – The leaves are boiled in water, serves as a kidney diuretic and to regulate blood pressure.

Artemisa - (*Artemisia* sp.) – Infusion of leaves in hot water and drunk, for stomach ache and flu.

Avellano – NGEFÜN - (*Gevuina avellana*) – Steep one leaf in boiled water and drunk several times each day, for diarrhea.

Boldo – FOLO - (*Peumus boldus*) – infusion of leaves or ground leaves in capsules, tablets, often mixed with yerba mate to moderate its flavor – traditional herbal remedy use of boldo leaf should only use aqueous extracts and not ethanolic extracts because of their high levels of the toxic ascaridole constituent – used for liver and kidney problems – also relaxes smooth muscles to prolong intestinal transit, serves as diuretic and as a mild laxative – also can work as an antiseptic, hepatoprotective, antioxidant, digestive, liver and bile stimulant, vermifuge, diuretic and abortive – eliminates intestinal gas, reduces blood sugar levels and ensures a healthy menstruation, also known as the hangover drug and alleviates the most distasteful symptoms of alcohol.

Borraja - (*Borago officinalis*) – Steep flowers and drink the water several times each day.

Canelo – FOYE - (*Drymis winteri*) – Infusion of leaves is placed on cuts to assist healing. Also for stomach problems and rheumatism. Essential oil extracted from the plant has insecticidal and fungicidal properties.

Cardo Blanco – TROLTRO - (*Argemone mexicana*) – Boil leaves and roots and drink infusion, for liver health.

Cedron - (*Aloysia citriodora*) – Boil leaves in water and drink the infusion.

Chamico – MILLALLE - (*Datura stramonium*) – Place heated leaves on area affected with rheumatism.

Chilco – (*Fuchsia magellanica*) – Infusion of leaves and small branches in hot water and drunk warm, as a diuretic and for urinary problems.

Chinita - (*Calendula officinalis*) – Infuse leaves and flowers in hot water and drink, for allergies, or make a paste of ground tissues and vasoline and apply to skin infections.

Congona - (*Diferonia inaequalifolia*) – Remove outer layer of leaf, heat, and place in ear for ear ache.

Coralillo – SINCHULL - (*Ercilla spicata*) – Make infusion of leaves in hot water and drink.

Corre-corre - (*Geranium robertianum*) – Leaves and roots are mashed into a pulp and used for baby rashes and foot fungus. If steeped in hot water the infusion is taken for hemorrages and for inflammation.

Culen - (*Psoralea glandulosa*) – Infusion of entire plant and drunk to induce vomiting, also used for stomach ulcers, diabetes, and intestinal worms.

Culle Colorado – KELLU KULLE - (*Oxalis rosea*) – Infusion of the entire plant is taken several times daily and is used for inducing the menstrual period and also to reduce bloody diarrhea.

Eter - (*Artemisia abrotanum*) – Infusion of entire plant is effective for removing intestinal worms and inducing the menstrual period.

Fui Fui – FWI FWI - (*Juncus chamissonis*) – Stems are boiled and the liquid is drunk several times daily, to initiate the menstrual period.

Hinojo – HINOKO - (*Foeniculum vulgare*) – Boil leaves and roots in water and are used to reduce intestinal gas and spasms.

Huella - (*Corynabutilon vitifolium*) – Leaves steeped in hot water and drunk several times a day, for cold and to initiate menstruation.

Laurel de Campo – TRIVVE - (*Laurelia sempervirens*) – Leaves, flowers, and bark boiled in water - for indigestion, colds, head aches, venereal diseases, and skin problems.

Laurel de Comida - (*Laurus nobilis*) – One dry leaf mixed with the food is good for digestion, or steeped in hot water and is good for the stomach and liver.

Limpia Plata – KELTRI LAWEN (*Equisetum bogotense*) – Entire plant, steeped in hot water and taken internally for bladder or kidney problems, injuries, and nose bleed.

Litre – LITHI - (*Lithraea venenosa*) – For rheumatism, submerge affected body parts in hot water in which leaves or branches have been steeped.

Llantén – PILUNHUEQUE - (*Plantago major*) – Leaves, either ground or steeped in hot water, used for closure of injuries, ear ache, ulcers, hemorrhoids, diarrhea, and head cold.

Maíten – MAGTHUN - (*Maytenus boaria*) – Leaves and seeds steeped in hot water and used for fever, injuries, intestinal gas, and constipation.

Manzanilla – POQUI - (*Matricaria chamomilla*) – Infusion of flowers and used for spasms, sore throat, and bronchitis.

Malva del Monte – DEFECONA - (*Hydrocotyle peoppigu*) – Leaves steeped in cold water and taken during the day , for fever.

Maqui – QUILON - (*Aristotelia* sp.) – Leaves steeped in hot water, useful for fever and bronchitis.

Matico – PAÑIL - (*Buddleja globosa*) – Leaves steeped in hot water, the water then used to wash injuries, the filtrate may be used as a dressing on ulcers and contusions.

Menta - (*Mentha* spp.) – Leaves steeped in hot water and taken for bronchitis or head cold.

Mil en Rama - (*Achillea millefolium*) – Infusion of leaves, taken for injuries, back aches, and hemorrages.

Natre – NATRI - (*Solanum crispum*) – Leaves steeped in hot water and taken for head cold and fever.

Orégano - (*Origanum vulgare*) – Branches with leaves steeped in hot water and taken for coughing, earache, and ovarian pain.

Ortiga - (*Urtica urens*) – Stem with leaves ground into a pulp and applied to areas with joint pain and rheumatism.

Paico - (*Chenopodium ambrosioides*) – Leaves and roots boiled in water and taken for digestion, intestinal worms, headache, injuries, and to initiate menstrual cycle.

Palo Santo – TENIU - (*Weinmannia trichosperma*) – The bark is boiled in water and used for lungs and kidneys.

Palo Trevol – TREVU - (*Dasyphyllum diacanthoides*) – Bark and spines boiled in water and drunk or applied as a compress for fever, wrinkles, and skin problems.

Palqui or Parqui – PALKI - (*Cestrum parqui*) – A common plant that was introduced from Europe. Leaves steeped in hot water and taken for fever.

Palto - (*Laurus orsea*) – Leaves boiled in water and taken for stomach ache, kidney pain, and to lower blood pressure.

Peumo – PENU - (*Cryptocarya alba*) – Leaves and bark steeped in boiling water and taken to improve liver health.

Pichi - (*Fabiana imbricate*) – Leaves and twigs boiled in water and taken as a diuretic.

Poleo – KOLEU - (*Mentha pulegium*) – Leaves in hot water applied as a poultice for injuries or the water taken for digestion and asthma.

Radal - (*Lomatia hirsuta*) – Leaves steeped in water and taken for head colds.

Romero – SASIN - (*Rosamarinus officinalis*) – Leaves boiled in water and drunk for bronchitis, coughing, excessive nervousness, and reduction of intestinal gas.

Ruda - (*Ruta graveolens*) – Leaves steeped in hot water and taken for stomach and menstrual pains.

Salvia - (*Sphacele chamaedryoides*) – Crushed leaves rubbed on skin for facial paralysis.

Sanguinaria – LAFQUEN KACHU - (*Polygonum sanguinaria*) – Leaves are steeped in boiling water and drunk to eliminate gall stones, purify blood, and as a diuretic.

Sauco – TREYKE - (*Sambucus nigra*) – Flowers are placed in boiling water and the cooled infusion applied to eye and skin infections.

Siete Camisas - LUN - (*Escallonia revolute*) – Branches with leaves boiled in water and drunk for liver problems and muscular pains and rheumatism.

Siete Venas – TREPÚ – (*Plantago lanceolata*) – See llantén.

Tilo - (*Tilia platyphyllos*) – Leaves and bark are steeped in hot water and taken for head colds and burns.

Toronjil - (*Melissa officinalis*) – Leaves and flowers are steeped in hot water and taken for nerves, insomnia, headache, and menstrual pains and as a poultice for insect bites.

Tusílago - (*Tussilago farfara*) – Leaves and flowering buds are steeped in hot water and drunk as a tonic and expectorant used to wash injuries or to strengthen hair in the last rinsing.

CPSIA information can be obtained
at www.ICGtesting.com
Printed in the USA
FFOW03n1812081015
17536FF